AUTUMN AUTHOR

BEATRICE FISHBACK

ACKNOWLEDGMENTS

Thank you to: Renie Onorato, Linda Robinson and Dana K. Ray: For the many years of being critique partners and my biggest cheerleaders.

Stephanie Gidney: British cultural insider and friend. Thanks for agreeing to take on this project.

To my Swanwick mates; Fiona Park, Jennifer Wilson, Allison Symes, Val Penny and June Webber: Daisy McFarland would never have been 'born' without your inspiration.

To Jim: You are the best; patient when I'm writing, caring when the words won't come and the greatest encourager when a book has finally been finished. Thank you.

AUTUMN AUTHOR

CHAPTER 1

A rope dangled like an uneven noose above the upstairs hallway. Its dark shadow moved in concentric circles on the tan-colored carpet. Slowly, the shapes drew tighter and tighter until they stopped altogether and the rope ceased its spin.

Daisy McFarland stretched on tippy-toes, grabbed the loop of twisted fiber and yanked it. An accordion-style, wooden staircase unfolded from the attic. The bottom step reached the carpet and opened access to a storage area beneath a pitched roof.

With a flashlight to guide the way, she climbed the steep, narrow stairs. At the top, something brushed her cheek.

Eek.

She hopped sideways and almost fell backwards down the steps. For some odd reason she had been jumpy the past few days.

A sweep of the flashlight revealed the culprit that had touched her face—a long string attached to an overhead bare bulb.

She pulled the cord. The light's bright beam exposed rafters, insulation, stacks of differing boxes and various sized spider webs.

Front and center were two boxes filled with clothing she'd kept in hopes that someday the garments might fit again, or the styles come back in fashion.

Perched behind were several crates of memorabilia from North Carolina that had belonged to her now-deceased parents. Some might say she was a hoarder since her folks had been gone for over ten years, but there were several things Daisy was unwilling to part with. Someday, maybe, when opening one didn't release intense memories and emotional responses, she could let them go. For now, they would remain lovingly at rest and sufficiently dust covered.

Daisy moved further into the cavernous space, stopped, tapped the BBC Radio Two app on her iPhone and stuck the phone into a back pocket before resuming her search.

She tossed aside plastic tubs of Tupperware that hadn't been used in ages.

Maybe she'd take the time to go through this mess in a month or two. When winter blahs settled into the English countryside and villagers hibernated. Yet again, how many of those same New Year resolutions and winters had already passed and the mess remained?

Local news by a British announcer broke her concentration.

Her ears perked. Even a news flash seemed amorous when spoken with an English accent.

As a cozy mystery writer, Daisy always looked out for new ideas. Headlines often sparked inspiration.

THE RECENT STRING of break-ins has turned into a heinous crime. A body has been found in the area where robberies have become a grave concern to local residents. The victim's name has been withheld until family members have been notified. Authorities are seeking further details leading to information about the burglaries and possible murder. A thousand-pound reward is being offered.

· · ·

A DOOR SLAMMED. The light bulb swayed and created undulating, eerie silhouettes.

Daisy jerked upwards and hit her head on the sharp corner of a rafter. "Ouch!" She grumbled and rubbed a growing knot with an open palm.

Had someone come into the house? Did she secure the doors before coming upstairs? Or had she left herself vulnerable to intruders? She hated to admit it, but the news had caused a wave of anxiety, making her muscles tense.

She glanced around for a weapon.

A rusty hammer leaned against a toolbox within easy reach. A large web blocked access. She cringed, slid her hand behind the webbing, grabbed the hammer's handle and held it high.

The biggest spider she'd ever seen dropped, landed on her arm and crawled rapidly along her skin.

Keeping head and shoulders bent to avoid the tight corner beams, she began a frantic war-type dance. The creature went flying and disappeared into a dark corner.

"Hellllo?" Rosemary, best friend and next-door neighbor yelled. "Daisy? Where are you?"

Daisy released a huge sigh of relief, dropped the hammer, rubbed her arms to rid the continuing tingling sensation and looked down the steps. "Up here. You scared the living daylights out of me."

Her friend arrived at the landing and cocked her head upwards. Rosemary's spiked hair—its highlighted coloring changed as often as the seasons—flashed tips of burnt orange in the light. A perfect shade for Halloween. "What are you doing up there?"

"Getting decorations and a costume for tonight's big do."

"There's no big *do*. We're just handing candy out to kids." Rosemary waved and directed Daisy towards her. "Never mind about that. Come on down."

"Let me find the box I'm looking for and I'll meet you in the kitchen. It'll only take a sec. Start the kettle and help yourself to a McVities in the cookie tin."

"Hurry up. It's important." Rosemary disappeared.

Daisy pushed aside Christmas boxes, found a large plastic tub labeled *fall decos* and made her way gingerly down the stairs. The last thing she needed was a broken leg.

"I should've asked you to help me with this." She plopped the heavy container on the kitchen countertop and rested her backside against the counter's ledge.

Rain splattered the window, leaving nature's glistening teardrops that paused and then slipped along the glass. The weatherman had promised clear skies.

Wrong again. Tons of rain this time of year was not unusual, but hopefully it would clear up in time for tonight's trick or treaters.

"Have you heard the news?" Rosemary nibbled a nail while gazing out the top portion of the blurred pane.

"What are you going on about?" Daisy stood upright and tapped the kettle with a fingertip. Cool to the touch. "I would've expected you to have a cup of tea ready by now."

Rosemary walked towards Daisy and grabbed her forearms tightly. "Listen to me, please."

"What in the world's the matter?"

"There's been a murder on Miry Lane. Number Ten."

"What? You're joking." Daisy stepped back.

"Remember those break-ins?"

"Wait. I just heard something on BBC Two about a body being found. For some reason, I figured it wasn't anywhere near Worlingburgh."

Rosemary released her. "Ten Miry Lane is that dilapidated haunted house.

Daisy sighed. "There's no such thing as a haunted house."

"Are you joking? Of course there is. Several National Trust properties bank their reputation on it. Anyway, they discovered a body in a freezer at Number Ten. Apparently, the electricity had been kept on but the company finally shut it off when bills hadn't been paid. The stink," Rosemary pinched her nose," was so bad folks living on the other side of the motorway called the police."

Daisy turned her back on her friend, shrugged and clicked the kettle button. "You know what they say? Visiting relatives, fish and dead bodies smell after three days. Besides, I can't think about that right now."

"What? What's wrong with you?"

"After those murders last year, I don't want to get involved."

Rosemary tilted her head as she reached into the cupboard, pulled out two china cups and saucers. The women knew each other's kitchens like their own. She plopped a tea bag into each cup, poured in hot water and quickly moved the tea bags around with a spoon before removing them. Then added milk. "Aren't you always telling me you need new ideas for your books?"

"I need new plot lines, but I don't need to get entangled with this latest murder. I'll just create my own misdeeds. It's safer that way." Daisy sipped her tea, glanced over the lip of the cup and gave Rosemary a look her friend had become all too familiar with—the one that clearly indicated she was done discussing murders. It was time to change the subject.

CHAPTER 2

*D*aisy stood on her front porch, tugged at the sweater lapels across her neck and blocked a small portion of the damp evening air. At least the rain had stopped.

A full moon, peering like a mammoth eye, glared down on those who scurried from house to house along Worlingburgh's High Street. Goblins and princesses, warriors and pixies tramped across lawns, crowded on porches and squealed, "trick or treat," seemingly unaware of the watchful orb. Smiling grown-ups plopped candy, chocolate treats, or apples into opened bags held at arm's length.

Like miniature flags, leaves waved overhead in the moon's luminescence; golden, burnt orange and red. All Hallows Eve—a night of jubilation for children who dragged bags of sweets back home. For others, an evening of night sweats, terror, and perhaps even a macabre murder like the one that had happened on Miry Lane. Shivers traveled along Daisy's back. The images of spiders and a body being found in a freezer were enough to make her shake and feel faint, both at the same time.

She closed the front door as the last of the young visitors left, flicked off the porch light and walked into her inner sanctum—the kitchen.

Rosemary, dressed like Gandalf from *The Hobbit*, had called it a night and slumped on a chair sipping Earl Grey. Her pointed hat, made from grey felt, laid crumbled on Daisy's desktop and left Rosemary's spiked hair flattened. The long robe, a hessian sack tied with a rope, gaped open and exposed her black shirt and slacks.

Daisy placed the bowl of sugary treats on the counter. "I thought Halloween was only observed in America, not the U.K."

"As a child, I heard about it, but didn't celebrate. Now it's as much of a tradition here as it is there."

"You did a fabulous job surprising the children." Daisy poured leftover candy into a Ziploc bag and rinsed out the pumpkin-shaped container.

"It was great fun and a good distraction from the —never mind, you don't want to talk about Miry Lane. Besides, it's getting late and this wizard's ready for bed."

"Don't forget your staff. Only you have the power to make it work." Daisy tapped the floor with the shaved tree limb, managed a weak chuckle and handed it to her friend.

"Where's Pillow? I haven't seen her."

"Probably mad. I tried to wrap a lighted lantern-shaped necklace around her collar, but she wouldn't have anything to do with it. She clawed it off before I had a chance to tie the thing on."

As if on cue, Pillow waddled into the kitchen with a look of total disgust and flicked her whiskers as if in annoyance. *Meow.*

"I'm sorry." Daisy reached down and scooped up the overweight, totally-white fur ball who could also be a shoulder to cry on and a friend in time of joy and sorrow. "I know how you hate being treated like a doll baby."

Meow.

Pillow tolerated the cuddle for a moment then leaped from Daisy's arms. It appeared the apology had been accepted and she'd received feline forgiveness. They were back on good terms.

"Thanks again for your help. The kids loved the tricks you performed," Daisy said.

"My pleasure. So, tell me, what happened to the handsome Detective Sam Decker? I had hoped he'd show up in a Tarzan suit and swing his Jane out to the jungle for a night on the town." Rosemary's eyes twinkled. It seemed they were both trying to make the most of the evening, in spite of the tragic news on the radio.

"I had texted and invited him, but he couldn't make it at the last minute. Said if he came, he'd be dressed as Darth Vader."

"Ooh, I like. Good guy dressed in bad guy clothing." Her friend giggled.

"You can stop now. I know what you're doing."

"You do?"

"Yes. Trying to lighten my mood and digging for information."

"Me? Dig? Why not? We're friends, aren't we?"

Daisy escorted Rosemary to the front door. "There's nothing more to report about Decker. We've had a few evenings out together since I returned from my stay at Victoria Inn, but that's it. Nothing of significance."

"You have that dreamy tone in your voice, though."

Daisy felt the rush of a blush along her cheeks. "I do not. Okay, maybe a little. But right now, he's busy. I didn't realize how much paperwork went into the closing of an investigation."

"I can't begin to imagine what's needed after such horrific crimes. Like those murders by Charles at the residential center."

"It's keeping Decker busy at the station even

though he's retired from the force. Who knows, he might be expected to have further involvement in this latest crime too."

"Such terrible tragedies." Rosemary held the doorknob. "Especially with John Symon's homicide."

"You said you hated him?"

"I did. He destroyed so many lives. It was Charles I referred to."

"Of course. I can't believe I misjudged his character. I considered him a dear friend, then discovered he was a murderer. I thought of visiting him in prison, but he's in maximum security. I'm not sure if he'd even talk to me if I decided to go, but it would be good research for a book. Search the mind of a man willing to take another person's life."

Rosemary shrugged. "Like I said, tragedies all around." She turned the handle, opened the door and smiled. "But, hey, we need to press on, and you need to get another date on the calendar with your handsome muscle-man."

Daisy chuckled, closed the door behind Rosemary and made her way upstairs with Pillow in the lead. "Okay, girl, get to bed and let me wash up before I turn out the lights."

Her chunky pet licked her paws and twisted to reach her backside. What Daisy wouldn't give to be so flexible. "Show-off."

Meow. Pillow jumped onto the bed, circled three times and curled into a white marshmallow fluff.

"What would life be like without you, girl? You provide me comfort at night with your presence just like the moon." She stroked the cat's silky fur.

Pillow purred softly then buried her head under the edge of the blanket as Daisy went into the bathroom.

Readied for bed, Daisy turned off the bedside lamp and pulled down her eyeshades.

She rolled into a fetal position and allowed her imagination to wander to a Detective Decker kiss. Her toes tingled with the sensation. If he saw her like this with eyeshades and flannel jams, he might have second thoughts about ever kissing her again. She giggled.

Meow.

"Okay. Okay. I'm going to sleep now." Daisy slipped into a relaxed state, moving slowly into a deeper rem.

A plaintive howl broke the night's silence.

Daisy bolted upright. She lifted one eyeshade. "What in the world?"

Who or what made that racket? And, at this hour. Daisy tiptoed to the window and peered out.

The moon, now draped behind prison bar-shaped clouds, shed long rows of white and black.

Trick-or-treating ghouls and goblins were long

gone but it didn't stop her from searching the dark swatches along the street and nearby park for things going bump in the night.

Another round of ghostly moans echoed across the road like someone or something in pain. A canine?

So much for a good night's sleep.

Creativity helped Daisy as a mystery writer, but it could also be her nemesis. Her wild imagination could snowball things out of proportion and often blew the smallest incident out of the proverbial water.

She flicked on the bedside light and grabbed the book she was currently reading— written by Dorothy L. Sayers—one of her favorite mystery writers.

CHAPTER 3

*N*ighttime noises evaporated and real or imagined bogeymen slithered away, disappearing into receding darkness.

To Daisy, daylight made life seem brighter. Better.

She stirred cream and sugar into a cup of coffee and sat at the kitchen desk. Her muse had been on strike recently, but with a new day and sunbeams filling the room, the urge to write again tickled her creativity.

Unlike the brutal beatings with a cane of John Symons and his niece and now a body being found on Miry Lane, her cozy mysteries offered no guts or gore. Building suspense and putting together clues to unravel who would commit a cold and calculating murder were her tactics.

She set the coffee on a Sherlock Holmes coaster, his face smeared from years of hot and cold beverages plunked on his cheeks.

Her fingers danced over the brand-new computer keys. After the tea spill that killed her last machine, she was thankful her latest model didn't cost an arm and a leg.

In every generation, the foolish and naïve had fallen for the kind, next-door neighbor who offered a wave and good morning, never realizing the same person could poison a supposed-friend without blinking an eye. How did one ever know if a murderer lived beside them?

Daisy sat back, lifted her drink and blew on the hot liquid. Were the words too sharp to begin a cozy? Balance in prose was essential. Another tidbit of training she'd learned at the annual Branick Writer's week. She missed her friends from Branick—the camaraderie, sharing Prosecco and friendly banter at mealtimes. It would be another few months before the Christmas event when she'd see them again.

Pillow had finished breakfast and meandered to a favorite sleeping spot on the small porch where a catchment of sun made for the perfect sunbathing space.

Meow. Hiss. Her pet's distinctive shrieks of defense came from the front of the house.

Meow. Hiss.

Daisy bolted to the door and yanked it open. Pillow zipped between Daisy's ankles, a blur of white fur, and dashed up the stairs.

Treacle, an overzealous Yorkshire terrier yapped with enthusiasm, jerking her leash as her two front paws lifted off the ground.

"I'm so sorry, Daisy." Mrs. Wendy Brown, purple scarf and purple jacket to match, held the dog's rein tightly. Her silvery, queen-style hairdo glistened in the sunlight and two rosy cheeks the visual victims of brisk air. "Treacle just loves your kitty. She's the only cat she makes such a fuss over." Mrs. Brown gazed at her dog with tenderness befitting a newborn.

Daisy put a hand over her mouth and feigned a cough, stifling a giggle. Treacle's haircut always made it look as if the dog were smiling.

Everyone in the village knew Mrs. Brown's assessment wasn't true. Her pooch loved every cat, squirrel, and any other creature with the same excitement as she did Pillow. But who was Daisy to argue with this grandmotherly woman whose smile matched her puppy's? She'd heard it said dogs resembled their owners, and in this case the theory fit the bill to a *T*.

Daisy faked a serious tone. "Treacle doesn't know better, but she does give Pillow a fright each time.

Maybe if you crossed the road when you see her on the porch, both animals would be happier."

"You're absolutely right. Sorry. I'll try not to let it happen again, but Treacle does have a mind of her own. Don't you, girl?"

Daisy shrugged with nonchalance. "Pillow does too, and I'm afraid she'd put up a good fight if Treacle dared come any closer. In fact, years ago a friend of mine had a dog named Scruffy who lost an eye due to a cat's clawing. A vet tried to save the eye, but an infection made it impossible. The half-blind animal was never the same. Walked with a limp and forever had a twitch."

"Oh, dear. That's not a very nice thought." Mrs. Brown pursed her lips and swung around as if offended.

"Good-bye, Mrs. Brown." Daisy waved to the retreating woman.

Her neighbor offered a backhanded wave.

"You can come down now." She coaxed Pillow who waited at the top of the landing.

Meow.

"Treacle's gone. I promise."

Her portly pet waddled down the stairs and made her way to the settee where she could look outside without worrying about a fearsome terrier who threatened to deposit cheerful slobber on her fastidiously groomed coat.

Daisy headed back to the kitchen, retrieved a banana from a basket, returned to her desk and stared at the words she typed on the screen.

...the foolish and naïve had fallen for the kind, next-door neighbor who offered a wave and good morning never knowing the same person could poison a supposed-friend...

Mrs. Wendy Brown? Daisy shook her head and chuckled as she peeled the fruit. Some neighbors were without a doubt innocent. Yet, hadn't the howling last night come from the direction of Mrs. Brown's place; the shadowy bungalow tucked behind a circle of trees?

She stopped chuckling. Charles had seemed innocent enough when she danced with him at the residential home, and he'd turned out to be a killer. Could her queenly neighbor also not be as she seemed?

Daisy leaned back, looked out the kitchen window and caught a bird's eye view of Mrs. Brown's back garden. From her vantage point, she could only see through a small opening in the trees as a six-foot wooden fence obscured most of the yard and house.

Daisy returned to her work in progress.

Even little old ladies with seemingly guiltless demeanors were suspect.

Weren't they?

Daisy didn't know much about Mrs. Brown other than what Rosemary had told her, "She acts sweet, but beware. She's not what she appears."

Was anyone how they seemed? Even Daisy knew hiding behind a façade of aloofness was her own defense mechanism. In reality, she was afraid of being emotionally burned again should she allow anyone too close.

Relationships were tricky. If she didn't give people a chance, she'd end up alone. Yet, being by herself had its advantages. No backstabbing. Nothing to worry about except listening to echoes in an empty house, eating alone and watching television.

Sigh. Enough ruminating. She placed her fingertips on the keyboard.

What could a mature woman do to a victim? The possibilities were endless and a certain village could be turned upside down by the least suspected person.

Noises from the basement of the spinster's house sounded like witches screeching with gleeful laughter as they stirred a bubbling cauldron of...

Daisy jerked her hands from the keys as if they had suddenly become sizzling hot. Dare she ponder to guess what wretched fare would be brewing in such a pot? Such reflections sent a trail of those spider-type goosebumps racing up her arms.

Daisy's muse had definitely returned. But where

in the world would it take her? She placed her fingers back on the keys and began again.

Movement outside the window, a shadow of light and then darkness, stopped her frantic keyboard tapping.

Mrs. Brown had opened the back gate from her garden, stepped out and looked right and left. Daisy kept watch as the woman lifted the brown bin cover, lowered something in and slowly closed the lid as if trying to be quiet.

Now why would her neighbor care if anyone heard her put something in the compost bin?

Mrs. Brown clapped and brushed her hands as she glanced around and then looked in Daisy's direction. She stomped a foot, put fists on her hips and pushed out her lower lip in defiance.

Daisy ducked behind the sheer curtain. What in the world was Mrs. Brown up to? She'd have to sneak over after dinner when the woman took Treacle out for her customary evening jaunt. Mrs. Brown was as reliable as Greenwich Mean Time and Daisy could set her watch according to the dog-walking routine.

Maybe the idea for her cozy wasn't too far off. Never, ever give someone the benefit of the doubt. Especially when they acted as mysteriously as the peculiar Mrs. Wendy Brown.

CHAPTER 4

*D*aisy's image in the hall mirror reminded her of hooded thugs whose photos were seen on covers of the Daily Mail. She pulled the black cap further over her ears and tucked her shoulder-length hair underneath.

Worlingburgh, mid-week after dinner, was as hushed as the morning following a rowdy night out at the pub for a group of yobs.

She quietly closed the front door behind her.

A horse trotted along a side road in the distance and broke the silence.

She tiptoed down her front concrete stairs, looked up and down the street, and circled around the back of the terraced houses. Rosemary had become her dearest friend since they first met in London and decided to move to Worlingburgh together. Neighbors on the left were never around. From what she'd gathered through gossip at the village shop, it belonged to a wealthy couple as a rural vacation home.

Much further down the road, on a very narrow alley called Miry Lane, a separate cottage was nearly buried behind overgrown hedgerows. Since moving to Worlingburgh, she had avoided it at all costs. Now she would make sure to stay miles away.

A police, yellow-taped *do not enter* banner blocked the road. For some reason, the crime scene barricade gave her a calm reassurance that she was protected from whatever lay beyond the tape.

Daisy made her way across the grass towards Mrs. Brown's back gate.

"Yoo-hoo." Rosemary was on her top floor back patio hanging laundry onto a taut line.

Daisy lurched, spun around, slipped and nearly fell.

Rosemary waved and leaned over the patio ledge. "What are you doing out there looking like Rowan Atkinson in *Johnny English?*" She giggled.

Daisy held a finger to her lips and mocked a "shush" as she moved closer to the house. "Keep the noise down, will ya?" She looked over both shoulders.

Rosemary leaned out further, "What's going on?"

She waved a palm downward motioning Rosemary to speak quieter. "Mrs. Brown."

"What about her?"

"I'll tell ya later. Just act as if you didn't see me."

Rosemary shrugged and smiled. "Fine. I didn't see you, Mr. English." She moved out of sight behind hanging sheets flapping in a slight breeze.

Daisy had lost valuable time. She glanced at her watch. Treacle and her owner would be back any minute. Dare she take the chance of getting caught?

She stepped towards Mrs. Brown's, the bin waiting as if on duty and protecting its valuable contents.

The long grass crunched with each step, and cooing wood pigeons added to the tension. Every muscle in her back tightened. What would she say if her neighbor reappeared? Although a writer, she wasn't quick with verbal retorts.

Be brave. Be brave. She swallowed hard. After all, what could an elderly woman donning the Queen's coif do?

Daisy lifted the lid with a slow creak.

Ahem. "May I help you?"

She slammed the lid shut as Treacle barked and bounced up her calf.

"Oh, hello, Mrs. Brown. Fancy meeting you here." How ridiculous was that?

"What are you doing lurking around my gate?"

Daisy straightened her shoulders and replied firmly, "I wasn't lurking."

"What would you call it?"

"I thought I saw someone suspicious dodging around the back, and I was just checking." Not a flat-out lie as Mrs. Brown herself had been suspiciously prowling there.

Her neighbor's brows furrowed into a deep V and a dark shadow passed over her eyes. The sweet elderly façade became a hideous sneer. "I don't see anything or anyone."

Treacle jumped up and down, yapping. Daisy liked dogs but they could be unpredictable and annoying. Cats on the other hand were always in control, albeit hissy fits weren't out of the question when Pillow wasn't fed on time.

"It's okay, Treacle." She squatted to calm the dog and to hide the tortuous heat of embarrassment rushing up her neck and cheeks.

Mrs. Brown didn't minced words, "Please keep away from my things. I won't ask you again. I will merely let the constable know what you've been doing."

Daisy rubbed behind the dog's ears. "You're right. I'm sorry. I had no reason to come over and check that you were safe." She urged her inner courage to take charge and straightened to look Mrs. Brown squarely in the eyes. "I promise never to interfere if there's someone entering your property, or double check that the noise I hear isn't someone trying to enter your house to steal your valuables."

"*Humph.* I doubt that was the case. But thank you for your concern. Come, Treacle." Daisy's neighbor spun around and walked through her back gate, the little dog close on her heels.

"Whew." Daisy headed towards home. Rosemary waited in her upstairs window with a wide smile, shaking her head and waving her finger back and forth and mouthing what looked like, "Shame. Shame."

She rushed into her house, pulled off the cap, lifted the black sweatshirt over her head and threw them on the sofa.

Pillow looked up at Daisy from her nestled spot and tucked her head under a paw. Even her cat was ashamed of her behavior. What in the world was she thinking? Going to a neighbor's and digging in the trash was beyond belief. Yet didn't every writer have to do research or some sort of sleuthing if they wanted to get into their character's head?

Daisy caught her reflection in the front hall mirror. "You cannot justify what you just did, no matter how hard you try."

"Okay. Okay," She spoke back to herself. A few tiny slivers of grey hairs shimmered in the receding sunlight. The fine lines around her mouth and along her eyes showed their displeasure. "It won't happen again."

"I would hope not." If anyone heard her speaking to herself they would think she'd totally lost her mind. Maybe she had. After all, what mature woman goes sneaking around looking into another person's garbage bins?

She moved away from the conviction of her reflection and went into the kitchen and the comfort of the laptop. At least there would be no talking back from her computer.

Daisy switched on the kettle, sat at the desk and tapped the keys to activate the machine. Nothing. Nada. Obviously, she needed to get used to the nuances of this new Mac. She used the shutdown option and put it to sleep.

A tremble darted across her hairline as she glanced out the window at Mrs. Brown's house. It had been colder outside than she'd realized. What a waste of time skulking outside when she could have been toasty and productive inside.

Daisy pulled the curtain closed and rose to make a warm pot of tea, decide on something quick for dinner and relax in front of the telly. Eventually, her escapade would be forgotten and she could get back to writing. At least she hoped so.

CHAPTER 5

*S*till attired in morning jams, fluffy slippers and oversized flannel robe, Daisy rifled through kitchen cupboards. Last night's sleep had been as restless as the night before. She dreamed of Mrs. Brown calling the police. Of being dragged away in handcuffs to the local precinct and seeing Decker's disappointment when he booked her for encroaching on her neighbor's garden and bins.

Daisy had her fair share of British police stations. An incident when she'd arrived in country, and interrogated about Nicholas Mark's death on her flight over the pond from North Carolina to London, had been enough for a lifetime.

She shook her head to rid the still-active nightmare. It was a new day. Plus, she was hungry.

Foraging through yet another cupboard, Daisy found a stale *Kind* snack bar and a bag of airline peanuts. A trip to the village shop today was a definite must. One could survive on K-rations for just so long.

Instead of heading upstairs to get dressed, she moved to the desk, coffee in a Harrods' cup and saucer set in hand.

Daisy blew a fine layer of dust off the antique tabletop and sat. Where was that housecleaner when she needed her? Most likely sitting at a desk in her pajamas eating a horrid tasting granola bar.

Meow.

Pillow moved in and out underneath the desk chair, brushing Daisy's legs with an upright tail. Their morning ritual consisted of her larger-than-life pet demanding food and Daisy wanting to finish an initial shot of caffeine.

She lifted the computer lid and stared at her reflection. Although not generally interested in vampire movies or the TV show The Walking Dead, in her current state she would make a good stand-in for either a zombie or a living corpse. Her reflection actually seemed to be shouting, *you look like a wreck. Finish that drink and at least go brush your hair and teeth.*

Meow.

"Okay. I'm moving." Daisy closed the computer,

swallowed the last of the beverage and carried her empty cup to the counter.

She climbed the step to reach Pillow's food stored over the fridge.

A few sprinkles of GoCat in the pet bowl and Pillow was purring like...well, like a fat, happy cat.

After scooping the exact amount of food the vet had suggested, Daisy stood upright and twisted sideways. Her elbow hit the coffee mug and saucer and sent them flying.

She released the GoCat bag, reached for the falling objects, and caught a handful of air.

The ceramic mug shattered into a thousand tiny pieces and the food mixed with the multi-colored glass in a layer of brown confetti.

"Oh, no! Not my precious Harrods' cup." It had been her first souvenir when she'd landed in Heathrow. Although on a limited budget, Daisy couldn't resist the chintz pattern and cutesy handle shaped like a heart.

Pillow shot out the room, escaped without trekking on broken ceramic pieces and had been spared being rained on by cat food. For that, Daisy was grateful. There would be no vet clinic emergency bills and Pillow wasn't hurt, which was most important.

Perched on the desk chair away from the catastrophe that had just occurred, Daisy observed the worse mess she'd ever made—at least in the past forty-eight hours.

Along with the floor being a disaster, the paraphernalia from last night's Halloween festivities were still strewn around the house. It was useless. That maid would never show up.

"Ugh."

Pulling herself up by the bootstraps...or in this case, by the straps of her fluffy bedroom slippers, Daisy moved past the confetti and went upstairs. The least she could do was put on some clothes to clean house.

With her hair wrapped in a red-checked kerchief, and donning torn jeans and a paint-spattered T-shirt, Daisy felt a bit like Rosie the Riveter ready to take on the army of disorder that awaited.

She grabbed a broom and dustpan from the closet. Where to begin? One bite of elephant at a time.

Daisy tapped BBC Two on her phone and began the herculean chore of sweeping.

Within minutes, the news was reporting on international crises and political mayhem before shifting to local information about the break-ins and the body being found. Part of her instinctively tuned in. But, common sense took over. She didn't want to know. Not any of it.

She silenced BBC Two, tapped the BBC FM

classic station and went on her merry way along nooks and crannies to the stringed instruments of Bach, sweeping up any remaining missed remnants.

Moving from cat food cleanup to dusting, the sweet smell of lavender polish tickled her nose. Although an autumn odor like pumpkin latte would be a more appropriate choice for this time of year, lavender was her all-time favorite no matter what the temps.

Sweeping and dusting complete, Daisy packed up the party favors and costumes. With the container labeled *fall decos* completely full and Pillow's orange lantern necklace propped on top, she made her way upstairs to the attic where the decorations would remain until next year.

The steps were as precarious as the day she'd retrieved the box. With careful maneuvering, she made her way into the loft.

Bam.

"Hello?" She set the box on the floorboards and glanced down the stairs to the landing below. "Is that you Rosemary?"

Silence.

"Stop fooling around." Daisy chuckled uneasily. "You know I'm already a bit skittish these days."

Bam.

"Hello? Who's there?" Dare she go down and investigate? The part of her that didn't want to hear the bad news from the radio station also didn't want to face the fact that an uninvited guest had entered her domain. Yet, waiting in a dark space with spiders creeping from every direction didn't seem a viable option either.

Daisy grabbed the hammer that was still sitting where she'd left it and slowly made her way down, carefully holding the hammer over her head.

Bam.

"Who's there?"

Pillow scrambled out from under the sofa chasing a mouse.

"Yikes. Ugh. Ugh. Ugh." Daisy jumped up on the couch and allowed her pet to do her job. Where in the world had a rodent come from? If nothing else, at least she knew the intruder wasn't some crazed robber looking to steal her prized coffee cup. If it had been, they would have been sorely disappointed.

CHAPTER 6

*A*s soon as Pillow had captured her living "toy," exited through the cat flap and returned empty handed, Daisy rang Rosemary. "Would you mind coming over for a few minutes, if you're free that is?"

Rosemary arrived in a flash. She currently worked from home, creating and selling clothing designs, and seemed readily available whenever Daisy needed her.

Daisy filled Rosemary in on the morning's fiasco.

Her friend frowned. "You need to be more on guard. It could've very well been a thief. Coming downstairs with a hammer...what were you thinking? We can't be too careful these days with—"

"Okay. Okay. I get it. With dead bodies.

Robberies." Daisy wrapped her upper body tightly with her arms and squeezed. In spite of knowing the miscreant had merely been a small mouse, she felt the need to hold in a chill of panic.

"Exactly. We don't have a clue what we're up against with whoever's breaking into these houses. Or if they have anything to do with the body on Miry Lane."

"I understand. I do. But, it was *only* a tiny mouse. In fact, I felt bad for the creature. Pillow's a lioness when it comes to anyone or anything entering her domain. You should've seen how she took on Treacle yesterday morning. Well, actually she didn't take her on. Pillow screamed up a storm and I had to open the door to rescue her from being licked to death, but that's besides the point."

Rosemary crouched beside Pillow, scratched behind the cat's ears and stood, a look of concern etched around her mouth. "You aren't taking this seriously."

"Of course I am. If I let my imagination run too far and too fast, though, I'll be swept away on a giant tide of fear. I can't afford to do that."

"You do it all the time." She pointed to Daisy's computer. "Right there."

"I think that's part of my problem."

"What is?"

"My imagination." Daisy nodded at her desk, proud of the surface's shininess that held the laptop. "Sitting there, coming up with ideas about mayhem and murder is starting to get to me. I even imagined Mrs. Brown might be up to something nefarious. How silly is that? Maybe I should take a break? Pick up something else like knitting?"

Rosemary shrugged. "Everyone lets their thoughts get to them now and again. Besides, you've always enjoyed writing. It's your calling. Your métier."

Daisy cocked her head. "I didn't know you spoke French."

"I don't. A very attractive bloke I dated did, so I picked up a few words along the way. Most of them I can't repeat." Rosemary's eyes filled with light and the corners creased from a smile as her face flushed.

"Now who isn't taking things seriously?" Daisy smiled in return. "Thank you for changing the conversation from someone coming into my house to sexy sounding French words." She winked at her friend.

Rosemary's countenance shifted. The smile turned into a straight line and her jaw tightened. "Daisy, you must make sure your doors are locked and windows secured. Come to think of it, maybe you should change the locks, order a Nest camera for the front and back. Keep the outside lights on. Anything that acts as a deterrent."

"Are you going to order cameras?" Daisy twisted the hem of her T-shirt between two fingers and sighed.

"I haven't decided."

"Let's both do it. Then I won't feel like such a wimp if I'm the only one living behind Fort Knox."

"It's a deal." Rosemary took a step backwards as if preparing to leave. "I've got to get back to work. There's an order I need to complete."

"How are things going? Do you like working from home?" She had hoped Rosemary would hang around for a little longer, but she couldn't be selfish.

"It's fab. I never imagined I'd be running my own business."

"There's that imagination thing again." Daisy giggled as she and Rosemary walked to the front door. Her friend always made such perfect sense and had calmed Daisy's nerves on more than one occasion. Whether dealing with the residential murders that had happened or Daisy's relationship with Decker, she was a tried and true person despite the now purple-tipped, spiked hair that looked so bizarrely flattering.

Daisy ran fingers through her own shoulder-length nothing-to-brag-about dirty-blond-brown confusion of style. Maybe she should cut hers super short. Closing the front door after Rosemary, she took a swift glance in the mirror on the way back into the kitchen and shrugged. Why not?

Between cleaning house and Rosemary's visit, Daisy had missed her opportunity to go to the village shop. Waning daylight and the darkening sky were enough clues that tomorrow would be another day and another chance to get food in the house. A frozen dinner would have to do.

Ding.

The microwave finished its magic. Daisy made her way into the living room, used the remote and clicked on the television. Pillow climbed up beside her on the sofa, sniffed the turkey and dressing glob on the disposable tray and lifted her nose in disdain. Her whiskers twitched as if implying the mouse was a much better choice than the food on Daisy's lap.

"Ha. You don't know a thing about grand cuisine. You eat dark balls of something or other from a GoCat bag. Besides, who knows how you disposed of that mouse."

Daisy cut a piece of turkey, popped it in her mouth, chewed the rubbery substance, and with difficulty swallowed the bite of meat. "Ugh. You might be right this time." She put the tray aside, tucked her legs underneath and sat back.

After several rotations through the channels, she

shut off the television. What shown on the screen was just as unpalatable as the food she'd tried to eat.

It seemed an early night was on the agenda. Maybe tonight she'd get a better sleep and Mrs. Brown would stay put in her home and not roam around in Daisy's dreams.

CHAPTER 7

*R*at-tat-tat.

Daisy lifted her eyeshades.

Rat-tat-tat.

She flung off the warm navy-blue and mint-green duvet, rushed to the bedroom window and peered around the room-darkening shade.

Just what she was afraid of—the dreaded autumn downpour. Miniature razor-sharp rain pellets struck the side of the house with a vengeance. And, today was trash collection day.

Her garbage already overflowed with the shambles created from cat food and china shards plus last week's trash. The question was, was it the brown colored bins this week and next week the blue, or the green? Cryptic collection directions seemed to change monthly to confuse customers and cause rubbish chaos.

Whatever the neighbors had by their curbsides would be a clue, and Daisy would follow suit. The bedside clock reminded her she'd have to be quick. The garbage collectors would be there in no time.

She rushed downstairs, pulled on flowered wellies over her pajama trousers, swiftly put on a yellow raincoat—aka Macintosh— and draped its hood over her head.

Pillow lay perched on the sofa, opened one eye to glance Daisy's way and closed it with disinterest.

"Lucky thing, aren't you. No garbage detail for you today or ever."

She unbolted the door, dashed down the front steps and around the side of the house. Rain peppered her face. She swiped the water away from her eyes and cheeks and pulled the hood further over her head.

Others in the neighborhood had their blue bins lined along the road like a row of ducks in a massive puddle.

With a firm grip on the trash handle, she dragged the heavy bin down the side path and around to the front. She arrived there in perfect time to see the garbage truck pull away, roll down the end of the street with its blinker penetrating the sheet of rain and turn the corner. She had missed them by mere seconds.

Daisy stomped her feet. A huge amount of water reached over the wellies and drenched her socks, pajamas and even the Mac. She was soaked to the bones, and now the rubbish would have to wait another week...or was it two?

She pulled the bin back around to the side of the house and muttered—several profane words regretfully intermingled.

Daisy could almost smell the faint and wonderful aroma from the timed machine brewing today's pot of caffeine as she made her way around to the front door. Sticky, wet clothes clung to her thighs and dampness infiltrated her skin. A cup of coffee would do just the trick.

She turned the front door knob.

"No!"

In her rush, she'd locked herself out.

She stomped again...several times. This time like a child who played in a puddle. Only she wasn't playing. The past few days had been one disaster after another. Her mind had become rattled with make-believe boogeymen around every corner and an attempt at securing her house from unknown intruders.

How had this happened? Normally an organized person who'd taught school-aged children for many years in North Carolina, she rarely lost her cool over silly things.

If she didn't have every t-crossed and i-dotted in her class notes fellow teachers would tease her relentlessly. Cool and even-tempered had been her motto then and remained consistent after retirement—at least in most instances.

Inhale. Exhale.

A few deep breaths and Daisy was able to restore a modicum of inner calm. If she remembered correctly, the kitchen window had been left unlocked. A habit she'd need to change after the recent break-ins around the area.

An outside rainwater bucket sat under the window, filled to the brim. She'd have plenty to use in the following days to water any late garden plants that tried to bloom in spite of cooler weather.

Daisy placed the hard-plastic lid over the bucket and stepped on it. Perfect. It created enough height for her short stature to shimmy up to the window's ledge.

She nudged the pane and managed to prod it open just wide enough. Daisy pulled herself up, wiggled and squeezed through the narrow space. She carefully avoided her desk and laptop and collapsed down on the floor.

Meow.

Pillow sat in the kitchen doorframe and licked her paws.

"Thanks for the help."

"Meow."

"Never mind. At least I got in." Daisy peeled off the coat and wellies and inhaled deeply again. She ran her fingers through wet locks and shook her head like a dog after a bath, leaving large droplets along the floor. Coffee had indeed been brewed and she was back inside. All was well in her world.

After a quick shower and wet clothes were tossed into the washer, she would stop and enjoy a cup of coffee. The preplanned schedule of when she wanted her manuscript finished, tacked to a cork-board beside the workspace, beckoned to be completed.

Daisy hung her Mac in the drying closet and trudged upstairs. Thoroughly cleaned and dried, she donned sweats, rubbed her hair with a towel and wrapped it around her head turban style.

Ding dong.

"Now who can that be?" It was still early and Rosemary was gone for the day to take her latest designs to a women's store in the next village. The few others she knew in Worlingburgh would never dream of dropping by so early.

She opened the door.

Two police officers—a man and a woman—stood on her doorstep and made their way inside without an invitation. "Are you all right, Miss?" The woman asked, the tone in her voice professional but obviously concerned.

"I'm perfectly fine. What's wrong?"

"A neighbor reported a break-in at this property. Are you the owner?"

Shivers traveled up from her toes to the top of her wet hair. The towel on her head began to unravel, and she caught it before it hit the floor.

"A...a...break-in? Here? And, yes, I'm the owner."

The male officer looked at his electronic notes. "Apparently a Mrs. Wendy Brown who lives behind this residence saw someone who climbed through the back window and reported it."

The heat in Daisy's face must have burst into a flame, she was so angry she thought her hair would dry all by itself. "What? Are you kidding me?"

"I'm sure she was merely concerned for your safety."

"Yeah. Maybe." Or maybe she tried to get back at Daisy for sneaking around her home dressed in black like a burglar to check out the trashcans. "She might've mistakenly taken me as a robber. I had inadvertently locked myself out when I took out my bins."

There was a quirk at the corner of the policewoman's mouth. The woman tried to either suppress a smile or had a nervous tic she had no control over.

"Would you like for us to inspect your home as long as we're here and be sure there isn't anyone besides yourself in the house?"

"Maybe you should. Just in case."

Arms crossed and fuming over Mrs. Brown's behavior, Daisy waited at the front door while the officers checked each room.

"It's all clear, Miss."

"Thank you, officers." She unwrapped her arms.

"We'd suggest you leave a key with a trusted friend or neighbor and be sure to keep all windows and doors locked. There've been several homes broken into the past few weeks."

"I will. And, thank you again." The officers left, and Daisy rested her back on the closed door.

Wait until she had the chance to speak to the intrusive Mrs. Wendy Brown. She definitely had a bone to pick with Treacle's owner that would most certainly go down to the marrow.

CHAPTER 8

*I*t took several cups of coffee to restore Daisy's mental stability. Fear that someone had come into her home and hearing it was her neighbor calling the police had sent her on an emotional roller coaster.

Reaching the apex of anger and feeling her neck veins pulsing, she needed to take charge of her reaction and keep things in perspective. Maybe Mrs. Brown really didn't know Daisy had crawled into her own house.

The rat-tat-tat of rain had slowed to a weak pitter-patter, while the veins on her neck returned to a normal pulse.

Sunshine peeked playfully into the kitchen as a tease. It had to be now or never to go to the village shop. She would get a few needed items to hold her over until she had the desire to travel further afield and drive to the larger Sainsbury's ten miles away.

Daisy made her way up to the bedroom.

Blow-drying her hair into smooth curls and taking off the lazy wear, she donned brown corduroy slacks, white long-sleeved top and navy down vest. A soft beige-striped scarf double-wrapped around her neck finished off the ensemble as she traipsed downstairs.

She retrieved a collapsible, blue-plaid, two-wheel shopping trolley with its zippered top and sturdy handle—a grand discovery she'd scored from a secondhand store—out of the front hall closet.

On many occasions, she rode her bike to the store, but today every muscle on overdrive with tension needed to be stretched.

Before exiting the house, she checked everything was locked up neat and tidy.

"Morning, Daisy." Rosemary waved from outside her front door. Beside her, Postman Rob held Rosemary's mail a bit too close to her friend's body. His right hand nearly touched her arm.

If Daisy didn't know better, she'd think they were having a rather intimate conversation.

Rosemary smiled broadly.

The postman moved away, walked down the steps, lowered his eyes as he passed and mumbled. "Morning, Miss Daisy." His fire-red neck fanned upwards into his face and along the edges of his ears into a thinning hairline.

"What was that about?" Daisy stayed put at the bottom of Rosemary's front porch.

"We were just having a chat up." Her neighbor nodded towards the postman. "He's a bit of all right, don't you think?"

"Him? You?" She didn't know whether to laugh or act incredulous. Rosemary wore clothes suitable for twenty-somethings on her over-fifty, well-shaped frame. Daisy knew her as a dynamic woman, gregarious and not willing to back down on her convictions.

Whereas, Postman Rob, thin as a rail and slightly bent over acted fidgety whenever Daisy watched him handle the mail. Daisy didn't know him well enough to decide if he might be a friend or foe, kind or the cynical type. He'd only ever acknowledged her with a nod or tap-to-his-brow salutation.

Rosemary kept her eyes on the postman as he continued down the street. "I'm tired of being alone. When that no-good bloke of mine wanted a younger woman, I thought I was over men. But, Robert, he's rather different."

"Robert? Ooh, that's does sound serious." Daisy giggled. "You're entitled to happiness. I've no reason to judge."

"Ta." Rosemary looked back at Daisy, shifted

from one foot to the other and pulled her multi-colored wool jumper tighter. "Looks like you're going for a shop."

"Yep. Need anything?"

"A small milk, please, for my tea. Let me get some change."

"Don't be silly. It's only fifty-pence."

"Thanks."

"See you in a few." Daisy pulled her trolley along the pavement.

Morning sunshine had definitely decided to stay put and heated the earth into a crisp autumn day. The air felt delightfully fresh.

There were four distinct seasons in Worling-burgh, and this, by far, had to be Daisy's favorite. Invigorating, bright and colorful. Winters were mainly dreary, dark days with little or no sunshine. Spring, although lovely with daffodils and narcissi lining the village green, always seemed short-lived. Summer tended to be unpredictable. Broiling one minute, chilly and damp the next.

Leaves pranced along the road as if gusts of wind swept them with a hurried hand. Childhood memories rushed in. Hot apple pie. Breakfasts of oatmeal sprinkled with cinnamon and sugar.

She skipped a few steps, the shopping basket bouncing behind her. To any onlooker, she must certainly look silly. Daisy didn't care one bit.

A car pulled curbside.

Detective Decker peered out his half-rolled down window. "Need a lift?"

Her childhood memories burst, and the warming glow of sitting beside a fire holding this man's hand slipped in. "What in the world are you doing here?" His presence disarmed her like no other. Even the rather dapper military soldier she befriended at Aldeburgh didn't offer the same shiver of longing.

"I just left Hill Game Resident Center and thought I'd pop over to your place for a few minutes. Looks like you're busy, though."

"If you call going for crumpets busy, then I guess I am." She giggled as she folded the trolley, placed it on the back seat and slid into the front. "But if you're offering a ride, I'll take it."

"I'd like to offer you a journey to the coast and have a picnic on the beach, but I've got to deliver this to the station in Delsey." He tapped a folder on the dashboard.

"Someday, maybe?" her voice squeaked like Minnie Mouse.

The detective offered her a side-glance and smiled. Their chance meeting at Branick during a Christmas event had been a grand encounter, never mind it happened over the dead body of June Fellows floating in a lake. When she'd gone to a council meeting in Delsey with Rosemary, they'd unexpectedly met again. Daisy didn't believe in coincidences. For some reason, he had been brought into her life. She wasn't about to take it for granted.

Two minutes later, he pulled up to the storefront and stopped. "Here's your destination, ma'am."

"Why thank you kind sir."

His smile faded as he caressed her cheek with the back of his hand. "I'm sorry we haven't had a chance to get together. I retired so I could do what I'd always wanted, but the council keeps shrinking the forces and every station is short-manned. Now they've asked me to help with another issue—the discovery on Miry Lane, plus complaints about strange noises in local villages to include Worlingburgh."

"Funny you should mention that. I heard some weird sounds Halloween night. Thought it might have been residue from the little goblins collecting candy."

"Could be, but considering the recent uptick in crimes, we need to take these things seriously." He cupped her cheek. "I'm sorry."

She leaned into his hand. The sheer touch of his palm felt like a hot toddy flowing through her bloodstream, a sensation she didn't want to end. "I had hoped we'd get time together, too. But I understand. Things come up."

"Thank you for understanding." He released her face and sat back. "I look forward to the next time."

"Me, too." She opened the door, leapt out and grabbed her trolley. The last thing she wanted was for him to see her childish tears. The old grey mare of uncertainty had galloped into her thoughts. Would they really have another date or had he just been kind? They already had misunderstandings about their relationship, but she thought they'd put all that behind them.

She waved a quick goodbye and scooted into the shop. Recently delivered fresh whole-grain bread and earthy odors of root crops propped on a shelf reignited past memories. Alongside the fond recollections, tears threatened, but she pushed them away, much like the wind had shoved the leaves along the road and rid them from view.

CHAPTER 9

"That's exactly what happened..." Daisy repeated her encounter with Decker to Rosemary. She couldn't simply drop off the milk from the shop and go home. Both expected a chat over a cup of tea.

"He said that?" Rosemary moved aside a pumpkin-shaped papier mâché centerpiece on the kitchen island, perched her elbows on the faux marble surface and cupped her chin.

Stepping into Rosemary's place felt like entering a mini museum of modern artifacts. Every room, painted a different color, had various types of novelty items; vases with overflowing flower arrangements and big, bright pictures adorning the walls. Whereas Daisy's home seemed simplistic, one might even say minimalistic. Cream-colored walls dotted with prints purchased from several charity shops and family photos were the extent of her creativity.

"He said we probably wouldn't be getting together for a while." Daisy perched on a red stool next to the island.

"He couldn't be putting you off, could he?" Rosemary's pout made Daisy cringe. "He seems like such a nice bloke. I'm sure there's plenty of twaddle going on that's keeping him busy."

"Not sure what he's thinking." Daisy shrugged.

Rosemary straightened. "I'm sure it'll be fine. By the way, I keep forgetting to ask what you were doing creeping around Mrs. Brown's outdoor bins? Getting ideas from her compost for your next book?" She giggled.

"I don't know what I was thinking." She shrugged." Just a silly notion, that's all."

"Why don't I believe you?" Rosemary's eyes twinkled knowingly.

"She got me back big time, though, I can tell you that much." Daisy reiterated the embarrassing encounter with the police arriving after breaking into her own home.

"Oh, dear. Sounds as if Mrs. Brown's lost the plot. I know she comes across a bit bonkers but doing that takes the cake."

"I think she was just trying to get even."

"Or, if we give her the benefit of the doubt, maybe she actually worried someone went into your house."

"I doubt it." Daisy checked her watch and quickly gulped the last of her drink. "Where's the time gone? It's nearly dinner. I better go home and put my groceries away. I've some catching up to do with my latest chapter."

"Is Mrs. Brown going to be eliminated somehow *Midsomer Murders* style in your next book?"

"Don't be silly." Daisy dare not tell her that their neighbor had indeed become a central figure in her recent novel. What writer wouldn't use an eccentric senior citizen as a main character? One who loved everything purple and owned a wild terrier that licked each cat she encountered.

Rosemary walked Daisy to the door and inhaled as they stepped outside. "Smells like rain. Again."

"It's definitely a season of change." Daisy sighed.

The twinkle faded from Rosemary's eyes as she offered Daisy a sympathetic smile. "Are you talking about the weather or your love life?"

"Maybe a bit of both. Before I go, how did your clothing design meeting in Delsey go?"

"Quite satisfactory. The shop owner rattled on about my patterns and wanted to purchase a few so I left there quite chuffed."

"I'm very happy for you."

Daisy meant every word of the heartfelt happiness for Rosemary, yet she sensed a niggle of envy as she dragged the shopping trolley along the sidewalk, up the stairs and into the house.

While unpacking groceries and stacking them on the kitchen tabletop, she stopped abruptly. Rosemary's demeanor towards her, about Decker, was nothing short of pity and she despised pity.

Hadn't she gotten over that ages ago? After college, she'd pulled up her bootstraps and moved on to become a teacher and now a wannabe writer living in Great Britain. She had plenty to be proud of at a time when her peers, who finished raising families, were now looking for renewed purpose.

Then why be so disheartened? Because of the detective? Since when did she need a man to give her life motivation and inspiration?

She slapped the counter. "Never."

Meow.

Pillow dashed from under Daisy's feet, the flash of a white lightning bolt as her pet made her way through the cat flap. The flap slapped Pillow on the backside as it moved rapidly back and forth.

She giggled at the cat's quick footedness when she wanted to get somewhere in a hurry. Most times, Pillow moved snaillike as if going any faster might hurt something somehow.

Daisy picked up her own speed while putting

away the bread in the breadbox, muesli and crackers in the empty cupboard and milk in the refrigerator. She was done. Done with being skittish, being afraid of her own shadow and flinching at spiders and mice.

She pushed out her chest, lifted her chin and belted out Helen Ready's song, "I am woman, hear me roar."

After finishing a few stanzas of the old 70's song, Daisy roared like a lion.

It was time to take charge of her life.

Her introverted self had been putting off meeting people. Mini encounters at the Women's Institute and trying her hand at yoga at the village hall were not enough to plant herself in Worlingburgh. To feel a sense of belonging in the community.

How would she ever be recognized as a writer if no one even knew who she was? What could she possibly do to make herself identified as a member of this village and someone who had gifts to offer that others might not?

Rosemary had inspired her with creating a brand of clothing and making a name for herself. Why couldn't she do the same?

The cat flap moved and Pillow slid through the slot, this time in slow motion as if she had all the time in the world. She plopped to the floor and closed her eyes.

Slow would no longer be a four-letter word to describe Daisy.

She sat at the keyboard and stretched her arms and hands before getting down to business.

It was time to come up with her own clever "brand." Bookmarks and other paraphernalia to hand out to those she met. Perhaps set up a table at the next village fete with her books.

What she needed was a logo to identify her as a writer. Perhaps a picture of a field of daisies, to match her name, along with some type of murder weapon.

Nah. Too simple.

She wanted pizzazz and that would take a lot of creativity. Maybe Rosemary could help banter around some ideas.

In the meantime, she needed to come up with a plan of action.

Daisy began typing.

Her heading read: How to locally promote my books and me?

She double-spaced and continued.

One: meet people through events held at the hall and beyond. She'd check the local Pilot and see what was on offer as entertainment for the next few weeks.

Second: Be brave. Act like a reporter and do her homework. Find out whose body had been found at

Number Ten. Not by putting her life in danger of course, but by becoming the snoop that would uncover the scoop. Surely that would give her notoriety in Worlingburgh and beyond

She gulped and swallowed any lingering fears. Perhaps then she'd be able to sell her books. Finally get rid of the stack she had on hand quicker than her cat flying through a flap when frightened.

CHAPTER 10

*I*f Daisy intended to uncover the story behind Miry Lane, and who had been discovered in the freezer, she needed to start from the ground up and face her fears. There couldn't be any more squeamish reactions to murders. Her heroine, Dorothy L. Sayers, must have been a brave sleuth or she would've never made such a great writer.

First off, she must decide whether to poke around Number Ten, or go through the village where folks congregated and ask oblique questions. The post office, village shop, hairdresser, fish and chip shop and bakery were perfect. For the time being, she'd pass on the pub. It might be useful later if she wasn't able to uncover anything helpful elsewhere.

As a relative newbie to Worlingburgh—most of the villagers had lived there for centuries—she hoped a few innocuous questions would come across as harmless ignorance.

With the day quickly coming to a close, it made the most sense to get up super early and start first thing. Excitement tingled in her fingertips, moved along her shoulders and down her arms.

There were days it felt as if she lived a *Groundhog* kind of life—the constant repetition of what had gone on the day before with no changes. Boring. Uninspiring.

Not tonight. With a skip in her step and humming a nameless tune, Daisy made her way to the bedroom. In the morning, things would be different. She imagined Decker just might short-circuit if he knew what she had planned. But he didn't have to know, did he? Besides, Decker's own detection work had become his time absorber.

A quick wash, teeth brushed and clean flannel pajamas donned, Daisy threw back the covers ready to hop in.

"Yikes!"

She shrieked like a six-year-old. First a spider, then a mouse and now some strange buggy-type thing crawled along the bottom sheet.

The tingles of excitement shifted to quivers of fright. *Ugh.* Bugs of any kind gave her the creeps.

A few deep breaths and mental reminder she wasn't going to let anything upset her emotional apple cart helped to refocus her attention on tomorrow's big day.

Daisy grabbed a Kleenex, gently picked up the bug, opened the window and released the insect into icy air. Hopefully, it could fly.

With the tissue tossed into the bathroom trash can, Daisy returned to preparations for a good night's sleep. She thoroughly examined the sheets before climbing under the duvet.

Pillow snuggled above Daisy's head and settled down after a few paw licks. Tomorrow offered a new and an adventurous day. No more *Groundhog* and no more frights or bumps in the night.

Daisy pulled down her eyeshades, turned on her right side and gently slipped into a deep REM.

Owwww-oooooh!

She bolted upright and waited.

Owwww-oooooh!

The howling sounds were the same as Halloween night. What in the world was it? A coyote? Cold sweat beaded along her neckline.

Within a minute or two, the noise stopped and the pleasant quietness of High Street returned.

Daisy laid back. In spite of the silence, she rolled over and used an arm to cover her ear in case the noise restarted.

Nothing. Absolutely nothing would break her self-will and determination.

Buzz. Buzz.

Daisy slapped the air beside the bed.

Buzz. Buzz.

She reached further, hit the alarm, opened one eye and double-checked the time.

What in the world had she been thinking to set it at such an ungodly hour?

Seconds ticked by.

The numbers shifted on the clock one minute after another.

Daisy sat upright and flung off the covers. She didn't have time to relax in the warmth and coziness with the investigative work that faced her.

There was a job to do. The same inspirational energy from the night before still flowed in her veins. If Rosemary had the drive to become a professional, why couldn't she?

Until now, Daisy only dabbled at being a writer. A hobby she'd started while still a teacher. Today, she planned to transition from what had been purely recreational activity to a full-fledged novelist. A writer known by others—at least by the few residents in Worlingburgh.

Pillow, one forepaw outstretched as if she might try and get up, raised her head a millimeter. She slid the paw under her chest before laying her head back down. There was no way her pet would greet the day with Daisy, especially not at this hour.

Cleaned and dressed, Daisy tiptoed downstairs. Pillow might only be a cat, nevertheless she respected her pet's desire for quietness.

Although it was too early to go to the shops, it wouldn't be too soon to take an initial peek around Miry Lane. In fact, this time of day couldn't be better. Mrs. Brown's early walk with Treacle wouldn't be for some time and there'd be little chance of running into her. Plus, hopefully there'd be no one or nothing else near the crime scene except the flimsy barrier that barred the lane.

Her thoughts jumbled from one scenario to another. Did someone still use the house and if so, who? Were the owners gone and had a vagrant taken up residence? Maybe there had been a fight, and the unplanned death had occurred between two home-less people sharing the house. Or did something even more sinister happen?

Wearing a heavy dark-grey overcoat and her hair tucked under the black cap, Daisy slipped a house key into her coat pocket before pulling the door closed. A handheld flashlight, along with a Swiss

Army knife with screwdriver and corkscrew were nestled in her other pocket.

Stars flickered and the dark sky bled red as the sun tried to reach its place on the horizon. The mantra her father said before leaving for work played in her mental disc...red sky at night, sailors delight...red sky in the morning, sailors take warning.

Cold, bitter air burned Daisy cheeks as she blew into her cupped hands. Where were those heavy gloves from last year's M&S sale? She'd make a lousy private eye as gloves were an essential part of any sleuth's outfit.

A car passed and disappeared into the semi-darkness. Its brake lights blinked like two evil eyes as the vehicle turned the corner without making a full stop at the sign. Who in the world woke this early besides mourning doves and foolish people like herself?

Daisy walked calmly down the street in spite of the fact her heart thumped a thousand beats per second. Her ears felt the timpani being played in her chest.

She shifted slightly and looked over her shoulder. Maybe it would be best to turn around and go back home. Sit at her desk, sip coffee, put on Classic FM and listen to Pillow snore under her feet. *Pretend* to know about murder and mayhem and let Decker solve the crimes.

Daisy faced forward—a soldier ready for battle—and moved ahead.

I will not be dissuaded.

Dim lights glimmered behind closed drapes as she passed rows of cottages.

Mrs. Brown's house remained dark.

Dogs cried in the far distance resembling wolves yelping in the night. Not that Daisy had ever heard a wolf, but she had certainly watched plenty of BBC documentaries to recognize one if need be.

The yellow police tape reflected growing daylight as it flapped slightly in the wind.

Daisy pulled out her flashlight, glanced around and checked no one watched as she lifted the tape and slipped under.

There would be no going back.

CHAPTER 11

*D*aisy used her handy-dandy flashlight and surveyed the face of the isolated and forsaken property at the end of the lane. Tire tracks, where no doubt emergency vehicles and police cars had traveled, left deep crevices that collected pools of muddy water from the recent storm. These were definitely not the type of puddles she or any child would want to stomp in.

She sidestepped the massive holes and directed the light beam slightly higher.

A rusty number ten hung sideways over a broken doorbell next to the front entrance. What had once been a green door now had mottled brown with speckled jade. To Daisy, it looked as if a lion had used massive claws to scrape off the paint.

Inside, on grungy windows, lacy drapes dangled

like strips of torn parchment paper. The sky's crimson color reflected along filthy glass and turned into a black-orange shade. Even the brightest daylight would be unable to penetrate years of dirt and grime.

As the sun stepped up over the horizon, its beams offered a fragment of life to the dead corpse of a building that had once been someone's home.

Daisy circled around back and avoided hip-high nettle along the path that threatened to encroach and sting her skin. She had been "kissed" by the wily weed enough times to stay far away from its spiky leaves. Rosemary insisted it made a delicious herbal tea, but Daisy couldn't get it anywhere near her mouth without dreading a sting to her lips.

Behind the house, dirty plastic plants were propped in broken pottery pieces next to short steps leading to a back door.

The low wall that surrounded a small, overgrown garden had several missing bricks and the remaining ones were covered with spindly English ivy.

Daisy walked up the slanted concrete stoop, cupped her hands around her eyes and peered through the backdoor window. Visibility was nil through the dirt-crusted pane.

She jiggled the door handle. Locked. Had she really thought it would be open? Even if she made it inside, what then? A strange, pungent odor seeped around the door and she held her nose.

Moving away, she walked around the path and returned to the front of the house.

Would past homeowners have left a key somewhere years ago? Back in the day when thievery wasn't common and most folks would've left their doors unlocked without worry, keys were hidden in case of an emergency.

With the flashlight, she scrutinized the surrounding area again along the nettled path.

Buried under overgrown grass and weeds, next to a casement window, the light revealed a medium-sized stone.

Daisy gave a gentle kick before she picked it up, half expecting something creepy to jump out.

The stone was actually a fake plastic rock anyone could purchase from the Pound Store. She flipped it over and opened a secret latch on the bottom. Which wasn't actually a secret. Anyone who had bought one of these cheap holders knew exactly where the key was kept.

Palming the metal key, Daisy paused before she slid it into her coat pocket. Although it would be considered police evidence, she envisioned coming back to take a quick look inside. Later, she'd give it to Decker. When next they met. Of course, who knew when that might be?

Maybe Rosemary would return with her? Her friend could be just as adventurous. Then again, it might push their relationship a little too far.

In spite of the cold, a string of sweat dribbled down her back.

Her iPhone alarm binged. A reminder to go home and feed Pillow.

No clues had been uncovered about who had lived in the house or whose body had been found, but she wouldn't give up. Not by a long shot.

As ANTICIPATED, Pillow sat in front of her bowl, a scowl of displeasure at Daisy's delay when she entered the kitchen.

"You know I love you." She knelt and rubbed the top of Pillow's soft head. "Give me one second to take off this coat and I'll get you your breakfast."

Meow.

"Got it. Don't take off the coat. Feed me. Right now." Daisy giggled.

Non-cat lovers couldn't understand the deep bond between a pet and their peep. Pillow was Daisy's confidante and friend. One who would never divulge her skeletons-in-the-closet, of which she had plenty.

Ding Dong.

"Oh, dear, GoCat will have to wait one more minute. I promise to make this quick."

Daisy rushed to the door. The Nest cameras she had ordered were promised to be delivered within a day or two. This was certainly much quicker than expected.

She yanked the door open. Her mouth dropped. "What in the world are you doing here?"

Mark Stranger, the retired handsome RAF officer whom she had met in the seaside town of Aldeburgh stood on her porch wearing a broad smile. "I know you weren't expecting me, but I had hoped for a much different reaction."

Flustered by her unexpected guest, Daisy didn't know whether to close the door and open it again in case he was an apparition or shut it and run upstairs to tidy up before letting him in.

"Is this a bad time? It looks as if you're getting ready to leave." He tugged on his striped cravat. It seemed to be Mark's particular "calling card" style as she clearly remembered him wearing one the first time they'd met at Victoria Inn.

"Oh, my goodness, how rude of me. Please, please come in." Daisy yanked her coat off and brushed down her hair with a swipe of a hand. "I'm sorry I'm in such a state of disrepair." She giggled like a schoolgirl.

"You remain beautiful to me."

He stepped into her safe space—a handbreadth away that took the wind out of her lungs.

She sucked in a nose-full of air. Mark's charisma had soaked over Daisy, and she didn't know if her legs could hold the weight of his powerful presence. She moved back slightly.

"I've made you blush. How ungentlemanly of me."

"Oh, dear." Daisy cupped her cheeks. "I'm pleasantly surprised, that's all."

"So this isn't a bad time?" His dimple deepened with a broad smile.

"Um. No. It's not. Um. You caught me feeding Pillow, is all."

"And how is she?" Mark and Pillow had quickly become friends since Mark was the owner of a lovely sleek grey male tom named Chas.

"She's fine but a little ticked off with me at the moment since I've kept her waiting for breakfast. Won't you join me while I get her food? I'm afraid the house isn't very tidy."

"I'd be happy to see your girl again, so let's not keep her waiting."

Daisy led the way into the kitchen.

Meow.

If a cat could fawn, Daisy was convinced her pet was doing exactly that. Pillow practically danced in delight at their surprise visitor and pranced around the room, tail held high.

CHAPTER 12

*P*illow fawned while Daisy fussed. After her pet was fed, Daisy put away stacked dishes from the drainboard, filled the kettle, wiped the counter with a damp cloth and gathered tea towels into a heap for the washing machine.

The last person she had expected to see was Mark Stranger. His military demeanor and lovely blue eyes that teasingly sparkled whenever he looked at her, had disarmed Daisy the first time he walked into the dining room at the inn. He had joined her at the table and they'd shared insignificant details about their lives while he ate a late breakfast.

"Oh, dear. Breakfast," Daisy said, snapped from her reverie about their chance first encounter.

"Did you say something?" Mark moved from his position by the desk and stood beside her at the sink.

"I thought perhaps you'd forgotten I was in the room."

She faced him, realized how close they were and retreated two steps. "Forgive me, I'm still in disbelief you're here."

The usual sparkle in his eyes flicked away and a shroud of sadness enveloped his face. "I can leave if you'd rather I go."

"No. Of course not. Please. Stay. It's dawned on me I haven't had breakfast and wondered if you'd care to join me. It won't be anything special. Maybe a couple of scrambled eggs with toast."

"How about some soldiers since I'm ex-military?" Mark's tease had returned.

"I know perfectly well what you're talking about." Daisy couldn't help but smile. "Those are for children, aren't they? Toast cut in slices to dunk in soft-boiled eggs."

"My. My. You've become quite the cultural insider." He smiled, his greying temples lifted and dignified wrinkles rose alongside them. "I would be delighted to join you. But only if I can help. If you'd like a CV of my skills as a chef, I'd be glad to provide one."

She tilted her head. "You've got me on that one."

"CV. Curriculum Vitae versus what you Americans would call a resume. Sounds much more posh, doesn't it?"

Daisy handed him a frying pan and giggled the schoolgirl-sounding jingle again. As a mature woman, she'd have to learn how to stop that. "I'll take care of the bread if you'll handle the eggs. Granary toast coming up."

Like a well-oiled machine, Daisy and Mark completed their tasks at the same time.

Coffee cups and plates of food on a tray, they made their way out to the small back patio and a wrought-iron table set. It had been bitter cold when Daisy had gone to the forlorn house on Miry Lane, but the weather had changed to the perfect temp for an outdoor picnic.

Daisy played with the eggs, moving them from side to side with a fork. She always felt awkward when eating in front of others. Instinctively, she knew how unattractive it looked when she chewed. Daisy's mother had often commented at mealtimes how Daisy's nose crinkled and her cheeks resembled chipmunks—a genetic trait from her grandmother. "It's not nice, dear," her mother would chide.

"What have you been up to since I last saw you?" She asked.

"Not much." Mark dove into his eggs, put a forkful into his mouth and seemed to savor the flavor as he grinned. "My compliments to the chef."

"You *were* the chef."

"Precisely." He chuckled. "Seriously, though.

There hasn't been much use for my services lately after the issues at Victoria, so I thought I'd scout you out."

"How in the world did you find me?" Daisy conjured up enough courage to eat a bite of eggs.

"Oh, you know us military and police types. We have our ways. Now tell me, what have you been up to? Writing? I noticed your computer in the kitchen."

"I'm trying, but it seems as if recent events have distracted me."

His eyebrow rose. "Events?"

"I'm sure you've heard about the robberies and now a body has been found not far from here."

"You do seem to experience interesting occurrences wherever you are. Those murders at the inn were quite bizarre."

"Exactly. Now I've had to order some cameras for the house and make sure it's always locked when I leave."

"If I remember correctly, you face your fears head-on." With one last bite, Mark's plate sat empty. A few crumbs from the toast were the only clue food had been on it. He pushed it to one side and picked up his coffee cup.

"I usually try and face my fears. But there have been strange noises going on at night and my neighbor," Daisy nodded in the direction of Mrs. Brown's house, "has been acting very strange. It seems everywhere I turn, something odd is going on."

"And then I show up."

Daisy felt the heat of a blush. "I didn't mean that at all. You turning up isn't odd." *Or was it?*

He glanced at her over his cup. The look morphed to a magnetic allure. "It was a risk I wanted to take, coming to see you. To see if that detective you were so keen on remained in the picture?"

"You mean Decker?"

"Yes, him. Or if there might be a chance you'd be interested in going with me to the cinema or a nice little restaurant I've discovered."

Daisy picked up her own cup, took a slow sip and looked down. Her heart would always belong to the handsome Detective Decker. She could still feel the back of his hand as it gently caressed her cheek. Yet he had made it clear, he didn't have time for her. For them.

Mark relaxed back in the chair, stretched out his legs, crossed his ankles and waited. Obviously, he was a patient man.

Daisy looked up at him. "I'd love to go for a movie or a meal."

"It's settled then. I'll pick you up tomorrow and take you to this wonderful Indian place. Say half six?"

"That'd be great."

A voice called from across the back garden. "Yoo-hoo, Daisy. I see you've found someone to protect both your house and mine." Mrs. Brown's mischievous grin was clearly evident as she lifted the lid of her brown bin and waved. Treacle barked wildly while tethered on the leash.

"What was that all about?" Mark asked.

"Never mind. It's the oddball neighbor that's been disturbing my muse, that's all."

CHAPTER 13

*O*nce the dirty breakfast dishes, cutlery and mugs were stacked back on the tray, Daisy arched her stiff back—a gift for traipsing around in the damp pre-dawn air.

"Is that my signal it's time to leave?" Mark winked, took the tray and walked behind her into the house.

"No. Of course not. What started out as an odd morning turned into a very pleasant one. Thanks to you."

"That's kind of you to say."

"It's true. Would you like another coffee or a tea? I've some writing to catch up on, but it can wait." It could wait until the cows came home, or the sheep in the field were shorn or whatever other animal's needs could be met. There wasn't a single reason she could think of why Mark should leave. Nor did she want him to.

"A tea would be nice, but I promise not to outstay my welcome. I'd like to hear what's been going on that's unsettled you so much."

"I'm being silly, nothing more." Daisy emptied the tray and clicked on the kettle. "Earl Grey or black?"

"White, please."

"Meaning you want milk with a black tea?" She smiled, not only at the language differences but how her guest seemed to enjoy testing her.

Mark returned the smile and nodded, quickly made himself at home and retrieved the milk carton from the refrigerator.

While her guest prepared the tea in a brown Sadler's ceramic pot, Daisy rinsed the dishes. She put them in the dishwasher and wiped her hands on a tea towel. The presence of another person in the house was something she could easily adjust to.

She placed teapot and biscuits on the cleaned tray. "Let's sit in the living room, shall we? I'll bring the cups separately."

Mark carried the treats and followed Pillow who walked in front of him as if directing where to go. Tail held high once again, she sashayed as if she'd entered a pet competition for the best-looking feline on the block. Daisy couldn't help but chuckle at her pet. What a character she owned and loved.

He placed the tray on a side table, poured tea and handed a cup to Daisy. She took a seat on an over-sized chair while Mark sat on the sofa and relaxed.

"What's been happening that's affected your writing?" Pinkie extended, Mark sipped from the china cup and scrutinized Daisy.

"It started Halloween when I heard about a body being found. Actually, it seemed to start before that night." She filled him in on other circumstances that had rattled her the past few weeks.

"Part of my silliness included spying on Mrs. Brown. Unfortunately, she caught me red-handed." Daisy felt her face redden with the memory.

Mark chuckled. "You didn't?"

She nodded. "Yep. I would swear she's up to something, but I haven't quite figured out what."

"And?"

Daisy reiterated thc fiasco of pulling her own trash cans to the curb. Being locked out of the house. How the police had arrived and revealed it was the snoopy Wendy Brown who'd called them.

Mark cover his mouth, evidently so he wouldn't laugh out loud.

"I know. I deserved it. For a brief minute, though, when the police first came, I actually thought someone had come in and it gave me the heebie-jeebies I tell ya."

"Heebie-jeebies? I can guess what it means but that's a new one for me." Mark pulled in his legs and sat straighter. "Surely an elderly neighbor with nothing to do except snoop isn't what's keeping you from writing."

"You'll be happy to hear I've turned a corner. About everything. Facing my fears and all that."

"I'm intrigued. How and why?"

"Rosemary...do you remember her? She came to the inn."

"Of course. An attractive lady with short hair."

"Yes. That's her." Daisy sensed a slight surge of envy at Mark's comment, but pushed the feeling aside. "She's started her own business, and is doing very well. Because of her, I decided to take my writing more earnestly, and create my own brand."

"Good for you."

"I'm dubbing myself a private eye and want to uncover who lived in the house where the dead body was found. Plus, these break-ins. Why the recent upsurge of houses that are being targeted?" Once Daisy started, she couldn't stop giving Mark all the details.

He rose, hands by his side as if standing at attention. His military bearing kicked in. "You will do no such thing." Mark's tone was soft but firm. Orders given to an underling by a senior officer.

Daisy stood. "I'm sorry, but I have to do this. No

one will consider me an expert in my field unless I take myself more seriously."

He stepped a foot closer to her. "Putting yourself in harm's way isn't a very clever thing to do just to prove a point. You've no idea who you're dealing with here."

"Think of me as a journalist. They have to go where the story is if they want to tell the world what's happening firsthand."

Mark moved a step nearer. "I can't imagine your detective friend would approve."

She shrugged slightly, aware of his closeness. A cloud of his aftershave enveloped her. "He doesn't know."

"Then let me help. It would make me feel much better if you and I did this together." Mark leaned towards her.

Rap. Rap.

Rosemary opened Daisy's door and peeked around the corner. "Well, well, well, it seems I've interrupted something very private. Sorry to intrude." Rosemary giggled. "Please, don't stop on my account. Daisy, I'll talk with you later." Her neighbor smiled, turned and the door quietly clicked shut.

CHAPTER 14

*S*itting at the kitchen table, their foreheads nearly touching, Daisy and Mark bent over notes Daisy had scribbled on a yellow steno pad. She walked Mark through the ideas she'd jotted down.

Her ultimate goal wasn't to solve the crimes as much as it was to write the perfect mystery. To have those in Worlingburgh discover who Daisy McFarland actually was—not just some unknown retired American in their midst.

Daisy had read years ago that Dorothy L. Sayers, the daughter of a vicar, had grown up in a small village in Suffolk called Christchurch and later became a renowned author. Daisy had a similar background. Only she grew up in the small town of Southern Pines in North Carolina as the daughter of a fearless lawyer who was well loved by those he defended. What Daisy wanted to uncover most from Ms. Sayers was her secret to success.

Mark straightened and gazed out the window before looking at Daisy. "Let me see if I've got this straight. You want to go inside that so-called haunted house?"

"Yes."

"How do you expect to do that?"

"I have my ways." She dared not tell him about the key quite yet. He'd probably put his foot down and demand it be turned in to the authorities right away. Daisy wasn't willing to risk that.

"Hmm. I'm sure you do." His eyebrow arched. He chewed on the inside of his cheek as if choosing carefully what he wanted to say next. "Plus, you want to hunt down would-be robbers? By yourself?"

She nodded. "That's the plan. So if you could get some helpful information…"

"Such as?"

Daisy tapped the end of her pen on the tabletop. "Addresses of where the break-ins have occurred. Once we have an idea of the specific areas, maybe we can narrow down potential suspects. Are they local teens or someone down on their luck? What's been taken? Why the uptick in home thefts?"

"Should be easy enough. Most information can be found on the internet these days."

"It's pretty crazy what you can find on there, isn't it?" Daisy detested social media. Once she realized what her fellow teachers revealed on Facebook, she was appalled and had every intention of keeping her personal details confidential.

"Do you think the break-ins are related to the body found on Miry Lane?" Mark asked.

Daisy pondered the idea. "It's certainly a possibility."

Mark rose, stretched and checked his watch. "I'd best be going."

Daisy stood. "Must you?"

"Chas needs to be fed and I have a few errands to take care of." He rubbed her forearm with his fingertips. "It's been delightful, and I look forward to dinner tomorrow."

Daisy's legs weakened. "Me. Too," she managed to squeak.

Pillow accompanied Mark and Daisy to the front foyer and waited until Mark had closed the door.

Meow.

"My feelings exactly." Daisy exhaled and saw her reflection in the hall mirror. A shimmer to her skin made her face practically glow. She smiled at herself and mimicked Pillow with a little Marvel Cat Woman type *Meow*, then giggled before going to the kitchen.

WHEN MARK HAD LEFT, Daisy hoped to write. Try as she might, the words simply vanished when she put her fingers on the keyboard. She'd originally been distracted by the goings-on around the village and then Mark Stranger stepped in and made concentrating even more challenging.

Tomorrow's big date was another distractor. Finding an outfit to wear would be as difficult as trying to solve a whodunnit.

Daisy gave up the ghost of creativity and proceeded upstairs.

Maybe her fairy godmother visited when she hadn't been looking and filled her wardrobe with several perfect dresses to choose from. All she needed was one, something to compliment her small stature and nothing-shaped figure.

To her, British wardrobes—aka closets—were a blessing and a curse. Limited in size, the number of clothes any person could own were minimal. And searching through different outfits could be a test in patience with the space between each hanger. Daisy moved one set of clothes after another. Each article seemed too summery or way too hot for semi-temperate autumnal weather.

After shuffling half a dozen dresses aside, she finally came across a black skirt and blue-grey striped blouse with a thin ribbon that draped the front. She'd forgotten all about the not-too-formal, not-too-casual set.

Daisy held the two pieces in front of her in the mirror and admired her reflection. The key was whether they still fit. A life of scones with jam and cream had been the dream of her lifetime. However, limiting the number of delicious delicacies had also become a must after the first year. The novelty had worn off, but the weight had not.

She changed out of her clothes and slipped on the skirt, zippering up the back of the material without a hitch. In fact, it looked quite flattering as she swung her hips side to side examining every angle. Next the blouse. It felt a bit snug, but the thin ribbon hid the slight tightness across her chest.

Daisy brushed her hair and struck a pose. A little makeup and a set of black heels would complete the image of confidence—she hoped.

Ding. Dong.

Pillow watched Daisy promenade around the bedroom with little interest, but at the sound of the doorbell her pet jumped off the bed and raced out as if she were going to answer the door.

"Coming." Daisy brushed the front of the skirt to remove a few pieces of white hairs that certainly belonged to Pillow.

Rosemary had probably returned to tease Daisy

unmercifully about Mark. She smiled at the thought. Her friend seemed to be having a liaison with the postman, so Daisy could goad her in return. Odd though, since Rosemary usually walked right in. The front door must have been locked. A good practice for everyone in these days.

Daisy practically bounced down the stairs. Rosemary could give her professional opinion about the outfit chosen for the big night out.

Ding. Dong.

"I'm coming." Daisy unlocked the bolt and swung the door open. A massive breeze brushed leaves that had gathered on the front porch into the foyer and fell at her bare feet.

"My, don't you look lovely. Going somewhere special?" Detective Sam Decker asked, as he held out a bouquet of flowers.

CHAPTER 15

*U*nexpected surprises often sent Daisy into a tizzy. Like when Nicholas Mark, a total stranger, died next to her on the flight from North Carolina. The whole experience with *Mark my Word Publishing* had unfolded into a wretched event from which she thought she'd never recover.

The move to Worlingburgh with Rosemary had ultimately rebuilt her self-confidence. Now, here she was facing an unexpected shock again. Not a Nicolas Mark-type-death but perhaps the demise of a relationship with Decker if he learned the truth of why she was gussied up.

"May I come in?" Decker moved inside before Daisy could reply. "It's getting chillier with the sun setting."

"Um. Of Course." Daisy crossed her arms as brisk

air blew through the house. Should she accept the proffered gifts and welcome the detective with open arms or quickly explain why she was dressed to the nines?

"Well, I'll be." Rosemary walked up the front porch and stepped inside with Decker and Daisy. "I seem to keep interrupting special moments."

"What's that supposed to mean?" Decker looked at one woman and then the other.

Daisy's face flamed with discomfort as she closed the door.

Her neighbor giggled.

Decker's questioning look clouded with a hint of exasperation as if he'd walked into the telling of a joke and didn't get the punchline.

Daisy swept her hand towards the living room in a wide gesture. "It's nothing. Please come in. Both of you."

"I wouldn't miss this for the world." Rosemary winked as she passed Daisy.

The detective walked by, his countenance drooping like the posies in his hand.

"May I take the bouquet and put it in some water?" Daisy took the flowers and went into the kitchen. Once they were placed in a vase, she put her palms on the counter, leaned in and took a few deep breaths. The beautiful bouquet needed water to live, and Daisy needed oxygen in the brain to confront this situation. Should Decker know she was going out with Mark Stranger or how they planned to work together to solve the crimes? Nope. That was definitely not a good idea. Daisy sucked in one last deep breath and forced a smile before she returned to the den of deception.

Decker rose quickly from the chair. "I understand you've had a visitor?"

Daisy scowled at Rosemary. They'd have a long talk next time they were alone. She faced the detective. "Yes, and it was quite pleasant, thank you."

"Why? Was *he*…here?" Decker's voice began with a painful tone, almost a funeral dirge type resonance and proceeded to escalate in intensity.

"He stopped by to say hello." Daisy swept the skirt under with her hands before sitting next to Rosemary on the sofa. She side-whispered to her friend. "Gee. Thanks."

Rosemary shrugged. "Deck asked. I couldn't lie."

Decker circled the room with panther moves, paused at the window and circled again. He stopped in front of Daisy and exhaled, hands clasped behind his back.

This was the man Daisy first met at Branick and who had stolen her heart. Did she still feel the same? He seemed to take her affection for granted. Appearing one minute and then disappearing for days as if he were a magician.

She pulled her shoulders back and sat even more erect. "Why shouldn't—".

"You're right." Decker put his hands up in surrender. "I've no right to dictate who comes into *your* home. I'm very sorry." With his right arm wrapped across his waist, left arm behind him, he bent slightly at the waist in contrition. "Please accept my apology."

If Daisy could've melted into a puddle of mush, she would've. Instead, she stood and faced him as he straightened. "There's no need to apologize, but I do appreciate it very much." One day that squeak would leave her voice when trying to express herself.

Decker sat on the chair. "I guess I'm curious as to why he visited."

"Yes, Daisy, why did Mark Stranger visit? I'm curious, also?" Rosemary turned on the sofa and looked up at Daisy.

She shrugged casually, and used a phrase often heard from her British friends. "Just for a catch-up."

"Nothing more?" Her friend prodded.

"Actually, I was telling him about the local crimes in the area. He's agreed to help me solve them." She practically spit the words out. Rosemary was right. Truth was best. There'd be no lies in her home, now or ever.

Decker and Rosemary rose at the same time and spoke simultaneously, "What?"

She stood between them, glancing back and forth as if playing monkey-in-the-middle."

Decker's tone deepened, his hands curled and on his hips. "You'll do no such thing."

Rosemary's London accent sharpened. "You can't be serious."

"I'm very serious. And it's both of your faults."

"Us?" Decker and her friend spoke again at the same time.

"Decker, you taught me in Branick when we found June Webber's body in the lake that I had the courage and strength to face any obstacle. Remember?"

"Yes, but that was different."

"How?" She asked.

"We were stuck in a snowstorm and had no other option but to use our wits."

Daisy ignored Decker's recollection and turned to Rosemary. "And you're always telling me to spread my butterfly wings and find myself. You've found your niche, and I want to discover mine."

"I didn't mean you should put your life in danger," Rosemary said.

"Mark has offered to help."

"Why him and not me?" Decker pouted slightly.

"I didn't think you'd be available since you've so much on your plate right now."

"But I have information that he doesn't have."

"I'm sure you can't share what you know with anyone, including me."

"Not directly. But we can certainly use some of the details without revealing anything that's not public knowledge."

Rosemary rubbed her hands together and smiled. "Now this should be very interesting. Two men both vying to impress my friend. It's a game of Clue with a twist."

Daisy and Decker looked at Rosemary as if she'd just entered the room.

CHAPTER 16

"*M*ark and I have dinner plans tomorrow evening." Daisy shifted from one leg to the other and tried to sound nonchalant.

"You do, do you?" Decker's voice shook, then raised an octave. "So when can *we* get together?"

Rosemary watched from the sidelines, her head moving back and forth as if following a close tennis match.

"We could chat right now." Daisy looked at her neighbor. "You're free to stay and join us if you'd like."

"Me? Oh, dear, no. I wouldn't dream of intruding." Rosemary giggled and walked towards the door. "You two behave yourselves. Don't get into any rows after I've gone."

The door closed and an awkward quietness permeated the living room for several minutes.

Daisy broke the stalemate of silence. "Have you eaten, or would you like some tea? Tea. Oh, my. Pillow. I keep forgetting to feed her today."

"Too busy with male company?" Decker's question dripped with sarcasm. He lowered his head. "Sorry."

"Please come into the kitchen while I give Pillow her food and we can dig around for something for us to have."

With tasks to occupy their thoughts, Daisy fed her pet as Decker scavenged the refrigerator for various items to toss into a saucepan and create a new recipe. Eventually, a spicy stir-fry appeared on the table.

Daisy and Decker sat across from each other. A vase of rejuvenated flowers, lit candles and two glasses of wine completed the ambiance.

Pillow had curled up under Decker's feet and purred. Daisy wanted to poke her pet with a toe and say, *Aren't you being a little two-timer here? You swooned over Mark just a little while ago.*

"What's on your mind?" Daisy asked. "You've been very quiet since we sat down."

"I realize it's my fault that you're willing to let Mark Stranger help out with this."

"It has nothing to do with you. Really. It was a

total surprise when he showed up." Daisy pushed her food around the plate. Here she was trying to avoid eating in front of someone again. Her mother's mantra playing once more in her mind. "Maybe we shouldn't talk about him anyway. Let's enjoy the time we have together. It so infrequent."

Candlelight flickered in the darkening room and it felt as if she were being transported back to when they first met.

"Of course. You're absolutely right." The detective scooped up a bite of vegetables and waited a moment before putting it into his mouth.

Daisy watched her companion and recalled his professional behavior at Branick. How he kept the attendees calm during that frightful snowstorm. There was so much she admired about him.

He laid aside his fork and reached out, covered her hand with his and tilted his head. "Tell me, how can I help you solve these crimes? Remembering, of course, the police are involved in finding answers to the robberies and murder. So, you and me trying to get to the bottom of what's happened might be a waste of time."

"Thank you for offering. We can at least give it a try."

Decker gently pulled her hand closer and kissed it with a brush of his lips. "By the way you look beautiful tonight."

She lowered her eyes. "Thank you."

A plaintive howl snapped the tender moment in half.

As Daisy jumped from the chair, Decker released her hand.

"What in the world's that?" he asked.

"I've no idea. It's happened a couple of night's now. First time was Halloween. I thought it was tricksters still roaming the streets."

"We've been told about noises being made in Worlingburgh, but I'd no idea it was such a horrible racket." He went to the window and pulled aside the curtain. "Seems to be coming from behind the house. Between here and your neighbor. Who lives back there?"

"Mrs. Wendy Brown." Daisy left it at that. No need to explain that her latest novel was about old-age pensioners being potential executioners.

The noise pierced the room again.

Decker grabbed his jacket from the hall coat rack and returned to the kitchen. "You stay here. Sounds like someone's being murdered." He left by the front door.

Daisy lifted Pillow and cradled her. She seemed to sense Daisy's unease and relaxed in her arms. On other occasions, Pillow always pushed herself out of Daisy's grip, bolted and hid under the sofa.

The back door eased open with a squeak.

She squeezed Pillow tighter and moved into a darkened area of the room out of sight. Had she forgotten to lock it? Would Decker be back before a potential intruder entered?

"Daisy?" Decker whispered. "Where are you?"

"Oh, it's you." Daisy placed Pillow on the floor and rushed straight into his arms. Her heart jack-hammered and her throat tightened. "I must have forgotten to lock the door and thought someone else was coming in. Someone awful."

Decker pulled her closer. "I'm so sorry if I frightened you. You need to make sure you lock your doors. Maybe I should stay if that would make you feel better?" He nuzzled her neck.

"It's just that you left by the front and I wasn't expecting you to come in the back. How foolish of me."

"Are you sure you want to go ahead with hunting down criminals and would-be murderers?"

Daisy pushed away much like Pillow would do when annoyed with being held. "What are you saying? I'm not capable?"

"I didn't say any such thing." He reached out to bring her back.

She softened her tone but stayed an arm's length

away. "I admit I overreacted when you came into the house. I need to have better control over my emotions."

Daisy flicked on the kitchen switch. The romantic atmosphere vaporized and bright neon light saturated the room. On purpose, she changed her intonation from fearful to fearless. "Where do you suppose that noise came from?"

Decker seemed to take the hint she wasn't to be trifled with. "I've no idea. It doesn't sound human. Could be an animal of some sort, but I've never heard anything quite like it. I'll have to turn in a report because it needs to be investigated."

"But that's what we're going to do, isn't it?"

CHAPTER 17

*W*ith one eyeshade lifted, Daisy checked the bedside clock. 9:00 am. Eyeshades and darkening window blinds were a gift from heaven. It could be midnight for all she knew or cared. She pulled the shades back down over her eyes and lay flat on her back.

Pillow made deep-breathing noises above her head, although it sounded more like snotty sniffles than a proper snore. Later, she'd have to check her pet wasn't getting sick. The flu Daisy had endured during the spring months had been awful. A long stay at Victoria Inn, although having its own difficulties, had cured everything that ailed her.

Sigh.

Yesterday. What a day. She clicked the day's events off in her head. Early morning trip to the vacant house. Mark Stranger at her door. Decker with a bouquet and Rosemary with hawk-like abilities arriving at the most inopportune times. It had been exhausting.

And exhilarating.

She smiled.

Decker had finally left after much persuasion. Truth be told, she would've loved to have him stay, but she didn't want to set any precedents. Regardless of how innocent it would've been, tattletale neighbors would be posting on the village shop board this morning that he'd spent the night.

Once Decker checked the outside racket and calmed Daisy's fears, they had chatted into the wee hours of the night in the dimly-lit living room. For her, it was all about the warm ambience. There were no resolutions about how best to proceed with the crimes, but he promised to come back. Today.

Her smiled deepened.

Ahh. Life was indeed a blessing.

Daisy jerked upright. She yanked off the eyeshades, flung off the covers and rushed to the bathroom to wash and change.

What in the world was she thinking? That meant *both* men would be here. Decker mentioned he'd come after work and knew very well Mark would be picking her up at half six. What to do? Where was Rosemary when she needed her wisdom?

Hastily dressed with mismatched socks and violet-colored T-shirt not coordinating with bronze-colored slacks, Daisy rushed downstairs and made a quick cup of coffee before going to her friend's house.

Daisy snatched her coat and yanked the door open, spilling coffee on herself and the floor.

"Good morning," Rosemary said, standing on Daisy's porch, a scarf wrapped around her head and tied under her chin like a grandma, or as the Queen often wore for outdoor romps. "Where are you going this morning? I thought you'd still be recovering from yesterday's activities."

"I was coming to your place." Daisy put the coffee down on the windowsill, picked up her car keys, grabbed her friend by the elbow and guided her out the door. "As long as you're here, let's go."

"Where're we going?"

"The bakery."

"Ooh, how lovely. Their millionaire bars are yum."

"No time for sweets. We need to go to the post office, village shop and butcher. Maybe the library," Daisy released Rosemary's arm, ran down to the curb while speaking and opened the car door. "Shall I drive? I know you like to be behind the wheel."

"Don't stop. You're a woman on a mission." Rosemary rushed to keep up and hopped into the passenger side. "I can't be gone too long, though. I've a Zoom meeting with some potential clients."

"Shouldn't take long."

Both buckled in, Daisy checked the speedometer as she shifted from first, second and into third gear. Getting a speeding ticket wouldn't be good for her driving record.

"So what's happening that you're in such a hurry?"

"I want to ask around if anyone knows anything about the robberies and the body being found on Miry Lane. I could use your help."

"Me? I thought those two knights in shining armor were going to solve them with you."

"Don't you see? If one outdoes the other, I could be in a real mess and lose their friendships. I wouldn't want that to happen. So, if you and I work on it, maybe I can divert a collision of male testosterone."

Rosemary burst out laughing. "What a problem. I'm lucky to have Robert chat with me while delivering the post. Imagine having two blokes fighting over you."

Daisy looked at her friend then turned her attention to the winding road ahead. "How's it going with him?"

"He's coy. Doesn't ever ask me out. Happy to flirt but that's about it."

"I wonder if he'd help us? As a postman, he knows everything about the village."

"He's pretty new to Worlingburgh, plus you don't want to add another man to the mix, do you?" Rosemary asked.

"You're right. I'm already in a pickle."

Daisy parked in front of the only bakery within miles. Although recently taken over by new owners, it was known by many for its

decadent works of confectionary. She avoided it at all costs. "When you come in with me let me do the talking. Be my ears and eyes. I'm going to act the dumb American as if I don't know what's been happening in the area."

Rosemary shook her head. "What do you hope to accomplish?"

"People love to tell others what they know, don't they? It's called gossip. And since I'm not legitimately from here, they can get away with telling me stuff, right?"

"We'll see. Many locals don't trust outsiders, so it could go either way."

The bakery window overflowed with cream puffs as big as clouds and pies that oozed fillings. A decadent aroma saturated the entire cafe as they entered.

"Why don't we get some coffee and a treat or two. Maybe the waitress will chat while she serves us." Rosemary acted like a child in a candy shop as she stared at the goodies on display behind a glass counter. "One of those, please. And those." She pointed at several items to include a large slice of carrot cake with thick frosting and turned to Daisy. "Shall we share?"

Daisy sighed. "Of course." Desserts were Daisy and Rosemary's kryptonite. Both succumbed to a sugar comatose a donut offered whenever they were given the chance. "I suppose we can head to the other places later, but we've gotta go before Decker arrives. Or Mark."

The tea and rich-tasting sweets exploded in Daisy's stomach. She sat back and moaned. Rosemary did a copy-cat and held her middle. "I don't know why I do that to myself. But, what a way to go."

Two ladies—mid-fifties if Daisy had to guess—entered the cafe. The first was short and squat. Too much tea and scones, Daisy guessed. But what right did she have to point out what others consumed after what she just ate?

Companion to the squatty lady was lean and mean and had the face of a Marine drill sergeant. If the woman ever smiled the skin-toned clay coloring of her face would crack and slide down into her combat boots. Not that she wore boots, but had on old-fashioned black shoes with inch-thick soles.

The women walked past Daisy and sat behind her.

With limited space in the cafe, listening in on another's conversation was inevitable.

"Tea's all I want." One lady spoke to the other. Considering the deep tone, Daisy assumed it was the Marine.

"I'll have a fruit cake with me tea. By the way, word's out 'bout the body."

Daisy's ears perked. She placed her forefinger over her lips. "Shh," she mouthed to Rosemary and leaned back.

"I 'erd he got a knife to his heart's wot happened." Marine mumbled."Likely he deserved it, nasty ol' bugger he wos."

CHAPTER 18

"*D*id you hear that?" Daisy blurted as soon as she and Rosemary got into the car. "Those women knew something about that dead body. I only wish they'd hadn't eaten so fast. That they'd stayed longer."

"I only caught bits of what was said." Rosemary buckled her seatbelt.

"How much time do you have before your call?" Daisy clicked hers and turned the ignition.

Rosemary glanced at the car's clock. "About thirty minutes. I have to be back by then. No later. Otherwise, I could lose an important client."

Daisy tapped the blinker and shifted into gear. She moved to the right lane and increased her speed.

A young mother pushed a stroller and held the hand of a toddler as she stepped into the zebra crossing—pronounced Zeb-Bra by the locals—assuming cars from both directions would stop.

Daisy slammed on the brakes.

Rosemary braced herself, palms on the dashboard.

"Whew." She tightened her grip on the steering wheel. "That was close. I was so absorbed in what those women said, I nearly ran through the crosswalk."

"I need some fresh air. You know I'm prone to carsickness and can't handle sudden stops and starts. Makes me nauseous. That's why I like to drive." Rosemary rolled down her window and inhaled.

Daisy slowly shifted the car into gear. "Sorry."

"Never mind. Now, what did those ladies say? One was shoving so much food into her mouth, I didn't understand half of what she muttered."

"Something about a stabbing. Then after they got their tea, she mumbled about family dynamics or some such thing."

"As you like to say, fish and family stink after three days."

"Do you think it could've been a feud between siblings? Or a Hatfield's and McCoy's kind of thing? Two groups of neighbors fighting. Maybe a Romeo and Juliet romance gone awry?" Daisy's imagination flew from first gear into tenth.

"Slow down, Daisy. Is this what sleuths do? Go

through scenarios and pick one that fits? Doesn't seem to work that way on ITV Drama."

"You're right. I'm not using common sense. It's the writer in me, I guess. I need to stay focused."

"What do you want to do now?"

"Are you game?"

Rosemary rolled up the window and combed fingers through her spiked locks. "For?"

Daisy checked the mirrors to be sure the coast was clear and shifted into first once more and turned left. "To look around a haunted house. I'll need to stop by my place and pick up a key."

"What in the world are you talking about?"

"Miry Lane." Daisy glanced at her friend. "I've a key I think will get us into Number Ten. If those women are right and a family is involved maybe we can figure out who used to live there. For some reason the police are keeping what information they have from the public. There hasn't been any news on the radio about the body since they first reported it. But, why?"

"Wait a minute. You have a key?" Rosemary shuffled sideways to face Daisy. "Why didn't you give it to Decker?"

"I actually forgot I had it. Until now."

Rosemary's eyebrow rose. "Why don't I believe you?"

"Trust me. I have every intention of giving it to

him once I get a quick look inside. Besides, when he showed up yesterday, I was so shocked I honestly had forgotten all about it."

Her friend clucked her tongue. "You're amazing. Where'd you get it? Never mind. I don't want to know. Of course, I'll go with you. But we have to get cracking. Time's running out."

Daisy accelerated. At least she was getting used to the narrow roads bookended by hedgerows. A street sign boasting of thirteen bends along a single mile had dissuaded her at first from getting a British driver's license.

Flashing red lights flickered in the side mirror. A police car rapidly caught up, its lights reflecting in the rearview.

She checked the speedometer, slowed down and pulled to the side of the road. "I didn't think I was going over the limit."

The police car sped past.

"Whew."

Another mile and Daisy would park, leave the car running and go inside for the key. They would be tight on time getting to the house and back for Rosemary's appointment so she'd have to be quick.

"Look." Her friend pointed. "There's a police vehicle over at Mrs. Brown's." Rosemary jumped out of the car before Daisy could put it in neutral. "I hope everything's all right."

Once parked and the vehicle locked, Daisy followed.

Mrs. Brown stood on the curb cuddling Treacle, obviously shaken.

"What's happened? Are you all right?" Rosemary rushed up to their neighbor, Daisy in close pursuit.

"Someone's...been...in my home." The elderly lady's voice broke. Her cheeks damp with tears. "Must've happened when I took Treacle on her walk."

The two police officers—man and woman—who had been at Daisy's house a day earlier—exited Mrs. Brown's. "You're right. It's obvious someone's been in the house. Everything's a tip."

"Oh, that's just my mess. I tend to collect things." Mrs. Brown blushed.

"Then how do you know what's been taken?"

"Treacle's treats are missing. Plus, I had a small television in my bedroom that's gone."

The officers looked at each other. "Mrs. Brown I'm afraid you'll need to find someone to take care of your dog for a little while."

"Why?" Mrs. Brown's eyes grew saucer-size. "Someone's come into my home, and you want me to give up my pet?"

"We need to have you come to the station and answer a few questions. I'm afraid we found some things in your home that need explaining."

"Oh, my. I've no one to take care of my little girl." She tightened her hold on Treacle as she looked at Daisy then Rosemary.

"I'll take her." Daisy offered. "It's the least I can do." Now why in the world had she said that?

So much for solving a murder before Mark and Decker showed up. How would she explain that their assistance might be more hindrance than help?

And, what in the world had the foolhardy Mrs. Wendy Brown been up to? There seemed to be more questions than answers.

CHAPTER 19

"*P*lease? Can't you take care of her for me?" Daisy, arms stretched, held Treacle towards Rosemary, while the dog yelped in resistance. "For just a little while?"

Rosemary crossed her arms. "I can't. I've got this appointment with that client interested in my designs, remember? As cute as the pup is, she'd be a huge distraction. I'm sorry, Daisy. You know I'd normally do anything for you." Rosemary offered a quick backwards wave as she hustled home.

Daisy turned and followed the officers as they escorted her neighbor to the police car, its flashing lights now turned off. "How long do you think Mrs. Brown will be gone? I've got an engagement myself tonight."

"We're not sure." The policewoman helped Mrs.

Brown into the back seat of the vehicle. "Does your neighbor have a contact number for you?"

"I've never given it to her, and I don't even know if she owns a cell phone."

The policewoman handed Daisy a card with the station's information. "You can ring later and inquire when she'll be released."

Daisy cuddled the dog while at the same time beads of sweat trickled under her arms.

Pillow was going to have a hissy fit. Plus, Daisy needed to get ready for Mark. Who would take care of the dog while they went out to dinner? Decker? She shook the thought from her head.

Daisy shuffled home while Treacle slobbered her cheek in thanks.

"What a mess I've gotten myself into." She unlocked the front door. "Pillow?" Her cat sidled out of the kitchen before she eyed Treacle.

Ears flattened, eyes ablaze, Pillow raised a paw with claws extended.

Meeeeoooowww. Hiss.

"Calm down. She's only here for a little while." *I hope.*

Meow.

"I'm going to put her in my bedroom." Daisy cooed in hopes of calming her cat. "Then, I'll feed you. And *Mark* will be here soon." Perhaps the peace offering of a meal and prospect of a good-looking man arriving would distract her.

Without notice, Treacle pushed herself out of Daisy's arms and chased Pillow under the sofa. She shoved her paws and nose under the couch trying to reach the retreating cat, her tail wagging in small tight circles like a motorboat's blades.

"No!" Daisy scooped up the dog, stomped upstairs and put the still slobbering Treacle into the room. "Wait here." The front of her shirt was covered with dog hair and the fabric stuck to her sweaty skin.

"Whew." Daisy swiped hair strands out of her eyes, headed back downstairs and lowered down on her hands and knees in front of the sofa. "You can come out now."

Pillow scooted further under the couch.

Daisy went into the kitchen, climbed the foot-stool, reached for the GoCat and loudly shook the bag.

Pillow magically appeared beside her bowl.

"I don't know how long we'll have our guest with us, so we're going to have to figure something out and play nice." She rubbed Pillow's head as her pet crunched kibbles. "Treacle can't stay in the bedroom forever."

Daisy's stomach growled and head throbbed. A quick glance at her watch showed it was past lunchtime. The sugar high from cakes at the bakery disappeared and her blood sugar plummeted. Something healthier was needed for her system if she was going to make it through the rest of the day.

Stacked cheese slices on a few crackers for protein and Daisy's stomach noise and head throb ceased.

The haunted house key glistened on the shelf as she put the crackers away. She'd placed the key in the cupboard in case any further unexpected visitors showed up.

Palming it, she went back upstairs and retrieved Treacle. The dog would need a walk and what better place to go than Miry Lane?

Treacle's leash had been attached to her collar when Mrs. Brown handed her over. Food and toys for the dog were retrieved by the police and given to Daisy before they took Mrs. Brown away. "Let's go girl. We're going to a haunted house."

Wind whipped in circles as she locked the door, shifting the temps from cool to a cold bite. She placed Treacle on the path and buttoned her coat. With a quick twist of the scarf to cover her exposed neck, they were ready to go.

Walking nonchalantly down Miry Lane, Daisy sidestepped the police tape and led Treacle along the rutted road. Puddles had since dissipated, and chunks of hard mud took their place.

Treacle took her sweet time sniffing every leaf along the way. At the rate the dog meandered, it would be tomorrow before she would be anywhere near the house.

"Please. Can you stop checking out places other dogs have been?" She gently tugged the leash. "I don't have all day."

Once they reached Number Ten, Daisy looked behind her to be sure no one followed, and made her way up the stairs to the front, being careful not to trip on the uneven concrete.

A shadow shifted behind the dingy curtain. Was it her imagination? She knew how well it could conjure up boogeymen at a moment's notice.

Her canine companion snarled.

"Hush girl. You'll wake up the dead?" *Ugh.* That might've been funny if she weren't standing in front of this particular place.

The thin and tattered curtain stirred. "Hello?" Daisy squeaked.

Treacle pulled at the leash and lunged towards the door.

"Is anyone in there?" Daisy gulped. Maybe a cross-breeze had blown through the house and shifted the fabric. It would make perfect sense since slight gaps in the clapboard siding seemed to indicate the house wasn't well put-together.

Daisy slid the key into the lock. It fit perfectly.

Treacle tugged and growled.

"What is it, girl?"

Once again, the curtain shifted and Daisy moved backwards. She reached for a railing. Something. Anything to stop her momentum, but only grabbed empty air.

She tumbled down a step, tripped over the dog's lead, and landed on her bottom at the base of the porch.

A shadow traveled along the window a second time and disappeared.

Blood dripped from Daisy's torn trousers. Unpleasant stickiness bubbled from an open wound on her kneecap. Her stomach did somersaults at the sight.

Treacle slobbered Daisy's ears and neck prompting her to move.

As Daisy forced herself into a standing position, searing pain shot down her shin. She shuffled unsteadily, being careful not to put too much weight on the bum leg, and took one feeble step after another.

The dog had taken ages to get to the house, and now she'd take ages to get back to hers.

One last glance at Number Ten before leaving the lane reconfirmed someone had indeed been in there. But who? And why?

CHAPTER 20

*D*aisy gingerly made her way over the chunks of uneven mud clumps. With each step, the knee throbbed as if it had been hit by a sledgehammer. "Ouch. Ooh. Ouch."

Pride cometh before a fall. No kidding.

Daisy's ego had gotten the better of her and she'd let sense and sensibility go the way of Jane Austen. What a silly woman she'd been to make a decision that could've caused serious harm. It was one thing to want recognition as a writer, but it would be another thing altogether to be acknowledged as a fool at her graveside if something worse had happened—like a broken neck.

Moving with difficulty past the police tape, she hobbled home knowing full well she resembled a hobo with her torn and dirty clothing.

Treacle took her sweet time and revisited every blade of grass, which worked fine for Daisy. She couldn't move fast anyway. Besides, this fierce pup had warned her about potential danger, and for that she would be forever grateful. Especially since she'd forgotten to carry her phone.

To keep the wound from gaping even more, Daisy kept the bum leg straight as she struggled up her front steps. What should she do about tonight? Mark would be ringing the doorbell soon.

Perched beside the door, a brown box with a *Nest* return address had been delivered. How odd that Postman Rob would leave a package unattended when there were so many looters around. Never mind. Obviously, the hoodlums weren't interested in small thefts like this.

At least she could secure her residence and not worry about intruders. Reports of thievery she'd seen on the local news app would make even the bravest heart take notice. Until yesterday. Then the updates seemed to stop. Had the police nabbed the guilty party or were there more burglars still on the loose?

Instead of reports on the robberies, highlights of upcoming Harvest Fetes now took front and center stage. Although harvesting of crops had occurred and church festivities offering thanksgiving for God's provisions, autumn celebrations were held around the country, weather permitting. In Worling-burgh, the Harvest Fete would be at the village hall at the end of the week. An ideal place for Daisy to display her books at a discounted price and meet visitors from surrounding villages.

Regardless of the news, she'd have to get the security cameras mounted. But, the growing throb that traveled up and down her leg reminded Daisy getting them installed was the least of her worries.

Once Daisy managed to jiggle the door open, Treacle made her way inside. Pillow would just have to hide from the pup for the time being.

Daisy picked up the box with as much care as possible, avoided bending her lame leg, and placed it inside the foyer.

She sat on the bottom of the inside stairs and surveyed the knee and trouser damage. Forget the slacks. They'd have to be tossed, and she would need to clean the gashed area thoroughly before deter-mining if stitches were necessary. One thing was certain, going out on the town tonight wasn't an option. Mark was expected in an hour or so, and it would take at least that long to make it upstairs, get the wound cleaned and covered with bandages. Plus take some meds. A couple of paracetamols should do the trick.

Hopping to the hall closet to retrieve her purse, she took out the iPhone and paused. Would sending

Mark a message ruin any future dates they might share? She had no choice.

Her fingers moved slowly along the keys. *Sorry to text so late. Not able to go out tonight. Bad fall.*

He replied immediately. *Do you need my help? I'd gladly come over.*

Thanks. I'll be fine. Let's make it for another night, shall we?

Absolutely.

I look forward to an evening together sometime soon.

Me, too.

Next, she texted Decker. There'd be no need for him to come over either.

And like a vapor, contact with both men disappeared into the Cloud. Canceling her date and telling Decker not to visit had been as simple as a few thumb strokes.

Sigh.

Daisy struggled up the stairs, into the bathroom and managed to pull the torn slacks off and clean up. She donned her jams, took some tablets and climbed into bed.

Whew.

Even though it was still early, she was ready to call it quits for the night.

Treacle pounced on the bed, her tail spinning on overdrive. Pillow joined the party and came up on Daisy's other side.

"Oh no." She'd forgotten about the pets. How long would Mrs. Brown be gone? Surely, they wouldn't keep her overnight.

"You and Pillow must be starving. But I'm glad to see the two of you getting along."

Waning daylight shed bars of dim light along the banister and foyer as Daisy made her way back downstairs to feed her companions. Days were definitely getting shorter and winter threatened to arrive sooner than expected.

It took some doing, but she made it into the kitchen.

A shadow moved along her back window.

"Yikes." She squealed.

Had it been a trick of the light?

Treacle growled.

Like the shadow at Number Ten, this one slithered away and retreated from view.

Daisy checked the back door. Unlocked. Had someone been in her house? She turned the bolt and made sure it was secure. Certainly, she had locked the house tight when she left earlier with the dog.

She took a slow review of the room. Was anything missing?

Things seem to be in place, yet something wasn't quite right. The kettle had been moved to one side. A book placed on a different spot. As if someone were looking for something but tried to be careful not to disrupt the setting. To cover their trail.

Or was she just being paranoid after what happened at the house?

Just in case, Daisy jimmied a chair under the doorknob like she'd seen in the movies and placed a glass jar on the windowsill in case someone tried to enter that way. The sound of glass shattering would alert her to dial the emergency number, 999.

Tomorrow she'd hire someone to put up the security cameras. She'd also contact the station and find out about her neighbor.

If Mrs. Brown wouldn't be back tonight, Daisy had every intention of checking out her property first thing in the morning. After all, she'd been given Treacle to take care of. Wouldn't she also be responsible for Mrs. Wendy Brown's other possessions? She might finally get some answers to what the suspicious neighbor had been up to and what she'd hidden in her bins. At least she wouldn't have to worry about any mishaps or accidents over there.

Meow.

Grrr.

She fed Pillow and Treacle and guided them upstairs. They would bunk together for the night. Once her bedroom door was bolted and the phone within easy reach, she'd feel much safer. Still, it would probably be a very long night.

CHAPTER 21

*D*aisy was torn—undecided between getting up, although the bedside clock only blinked 5:00 a.m, or trying to go back to sleep? Stay where it was warm and safe or move and make a pot of coffee before traipsing over to Mrs. Brown's?

Pillow had slept above Daisy's head, while Treacle found a comfy spot at the foot of the bed. A miraculous transition had somehow occurred. The two of them figured out they weren't enemies.

But how about her? Did she have an enemy? Had someone been in her house? There seemed a very real possibility that an intruder had been lurking out back last night, but she was too chicken to check. What kind of P.I. was she?

In spite of the cozy duvet, a tremor traveled up

her spine and she shivered. Daisy drew the quilt closer and tucked it tightly under her chin.

What could she possibly own that anyone would want? Her computer hadn't been nicked, and the few pieces of jewelry her mother had bequeathed weren't taken. Otherwise, her charity shop decor was not a burglar's ideal steal. So what were they looking for?

5:15. There was no way she'd be going back to sleep. With resignation, she removed the covers and switched on the bedside lamp. The pulsating sensation around her kneecap seemed to have subsided. Taking meds every four hours did the trick.

Daisy put on her bathrobe and slippers and left the pooch and feline to their sweet dreams. They'd be downstairs soon enough slobbering all over the kitchen floor wanting to be fed.

A disquieting atmosphere permeated the kitchen as she edged her way into the room.

She flipped on the under-counter lights. They normally offered a subtle tone of snugness and comfort, but this morning nothing seemed to settle her unease. Even the smell of brewing java that dripped and gurgled through the aged machine offered no consolation for her nerves.

Daisy peered out the window beside her computer. The poor desk chair had forgotten who she was since she hadn't been anywhere near it for what seemed like ages.

Ambitious writing goals on the cork board made a mockery of how far behind she was in achieving her objectives.

She ignored the call of the keyboard and looked out the window again. Pitch black. A low layer of fog hung below the streetlight and thwarted its attempt to illumine the circle of houses. If a setting could scream otherworldly, this was it. She drew her robe closer and lifted the collar around the nape of her neck.

A cup of coffee and bowl of hot porridge, and Daisy's bloodstream trickled to life, her muscles warming to the food and liquid.

She went upstairs, took care not to disturb the animals still snug in bed, and swapped out her pajamas for warm corduroy trousers. Last, she donned a heavy sweater and pocketed her phone.

In the foyer, she exchanged slippers for wellies and put on the Macintosh. With the handy flashlight and Swiss Army knife, a new James Bond was born. Time to find out what Mrs. Wendy Brown at been up to these past few weeks.

Leaving by the back door, Daisy snapped fully awake when the morning air slapped her face. After double-checking the door was locked, she clicked on the flashlight, keeping its beam lowered to the ground. The last thing she needed was to trip and fall again.

With careful strides, she walked across the lawn and approached her neighbor's back gate. The bins were lined along the fence like soldiers in formation. Brown. Green. Blue. Which one had Mrs. Brown been sneaking things into? Daisy would look inside them once she circled the house and determined if a window or door had been left open. If anyone saw her she'd simply say she was checking the property to be sure it was secure.

The back gate screeched. At least that's how it sounded to Daisy—her five senses heightened to their full potential.

Mrs. Brown's backyard was a jumble of rusty and broken garden furniture pieces. Various-sized ugly gnomes and several dead plants—the perfect setting for a Halloween gathering. How could someone who dressed so fastidiously and with her hair in perfect shape have such a tip in the yard? Moving the light's beam across the untidy heap nearly dissuaded her from going any further. Almost.

Daisy pressed on.

So far, there'd been zero success in her endeavors to solve the recent crimes. The only thing she knew for certain was the dead body had been knifed and stuffed in a refrigerator. Someone had been in

Number Ten, and perhaps that same person had pillaged the houses in the area.

Did Mrs. Brown know any of the details? With her age, and being a life-long local, she would know more than most. Besides the fact that she walked the streets morning, noon and evening with Treacle. Wouldn't she be able to figure out who was at home or not with an easy glance into windows as she went on her way? Yet, why would Mrs. Brown call the police and report a break-in? To take them off her scent as a possible suspect?

Maybe Daisy's latest novel hadn't been too far off. One could never take for granted that a nice, elderly neighbor was indeed who she appeared to be.

Making her way through the clutter, she tried the back door. Locked. Moved to a side window. Closed. Next one. Daisy couldn't budge it. Front door. Bolted. On the other side of the house, two more windows were the last chance of getting inside. The first—no joy. She scanned the final one with the flashlight. Luck was on her side as it appeared slightly ajar. With experience climbing into her own back window, Daisy was already a pro as she shimmied inside.

If she thought the backyard was a mess, she was unprepared for what greeted her inside.

CHAPTER 22

*I*n what appeared to be the main bedroom, a maze of a gargantuan mess faced Daisy.

Surely, the whole house couldn't be this disastrous. She sidestepped through the chaos.

Having watched television programs about hoarders, Daisy was certain this fit the bill to a *T*. She'd thought her few possessions in the attic were too much to keep. Mrs. Brown's place would be ideal in a primetime slot on the TV series.

Regardless of what Mrs. Brown might have done, it was obvious she needed help. According to the show, evidence had proven severe loneliness could trigger such behavior. Her neighbor had acted defensively and haughty at times, but perhaps it was a coverup for a much deeper problem.

Daisy shook her head. What was she thinking? This lady might be responsible for invading other's properties and taking what didn't belong to her. Could Mrs. Brown be involved with the murder, too? Then, of course, there was that old adage of being innocent until proven guilty. She'd have to be careful not to judge. After all, others had judged her as a teacher and it had taken a toll on her self-worth.

Another sweep of the flashlight, and Daisy navigated through a narrow path of rubbish towards a doorframe.

Paper rustled.

She stopped short.

What was that?

The pile of balled-up dresses and clothing shifted as if a mole were burrowing deep within.

Meow. Meoooww.

A tabby cat bolted out from under the clutter and screamed its way into another part of the house.

"Yikes!" She stumbled over an ottoman.

Her neighbor owned a feline? No wonder Treacle was so comfortable with Pillow.

Daisy took her time as she entered a narrow hallway.

Meow.

Another cat, thick black fur and eerie, with glassy-looking bright green eyes that glowed in her flashlight, stood front and center—a protector with its back-of-the-neck hairs spiked in fear or anger. Fully aware of Pillow's behavior when confronted by a foe, Daisy squatted in front of the animal, patted her hands down and spoke calmly. "Shh. Shh. It's all right. I'm not going to hurt you."

She straightened, stepped forward and the animal shot past her legs and disappeared into the bedroom maze.

Were these animals the source of noises at night? If the weather had been just right and Mrs. Brown's windows slightly open, the sound could travel across the lawns as if through a megaphone. Especially if there were more cats hidden throughout the house.

Peering to the left, Daisy once again used her light to guide the way. The sitting room seemed reasonably tidy compared to other parts, although stacks of papers and books towered in one corner of the room. An empty spot on a waist-high pine box showed thick dust around a clean area where a television had most likely sat, its disappearance supposedly the reason Mrs. Brown had called the police in the first place.

She made her way around another corner, paused and listened.

Had someone coughed right outside the front door?

Daisy tuned off the flashlight and held her breath as the sound of a key wiggled in the lock.

She retreated into a corner of the sitting room.

If Mrs. Brown were returning, Daisy would have plenty of explaining to do. Her neighbor had been ticked off enough at Daisy when she merely peeked inside her bins.

A male voice spoke to another unseen person. "Let's make it quick."

"She doesn't have a clue." The other voice could've been either a man or woman since their loud whispers were muffled through the wall.

Daisy took short, quiet breaths to settle her pounding heart, as she pushed back further into the wall where a shield of darkness kept her well hidden. Throbbing resumed around her kneecap and down her shin—the medication quickly wearing off.

"The police did us a favor keeping Brown for the night. Calling the station and squealing the old lady could've been the thief was a brilliant idea of yours. We can move the steals from Miry to here with her gone." The man said.

"Once they'd finished clearing out the body from Number Ten it would've been the perfect place to hide the stash, but that snoopy American nearly caught us so we had to do something quick."

"This place is perfect."

"Brown'll never suspect she's safekeeping this loot. She's so much gubbins, she wouldn't know it doesn't belong to her." The female sounding intruder cackled.

Who were these two? One voice sounded familiar, but it was difficult to tell. Crooks for certain.

"How much more we gotta move?" The man asked.

"Couple more trips."

"I'll wait here and keep an eye on things in case the missus of the house returns from the station. If she does, I'll text ya."

The front door shut and the lone invader hummed his way into the kitchen. The kettle clicked and a familiar hiss of boiling water traveled into the corner where Daisy waited.

Dare she try and run? Or tiptoe out the way she'd entered?

Humming intensified as the man walked into the sitting room.

She held her breath.

After a quick circle as if inspecting the room, he returned the way he'd entered from the kitchen.

Aroma of tea brewing wafted into the sitting room. Daisy licked her lips. She'd die for a cuppa right about now. Or a drink of water—thirst triggered by fear threatened to overwhelm her.

On the other hand, she needed a bathroom badly. How long could she hold on and what would these two do if they discovered her?

Panic replaced fear. Perspiration saturated the back of her sweater and slacks. She couldn't outrun these hoodlums with a bum leg. Her best course of action would be to wait it out. But for how long?

The stranger returned to the room.

Daisy strained her neck. Maybe she could get a good look and identify him.

Plopping down on the torn, saggy flowered chair only meters away, he removed his cap.

She inhaled and covered her mouth.

The man turned in her direction. Had he heard the sound?

CHAPTER 23

*W*as the intruder really who Daisy thought it might be? Although the shape of his head seemed to be right, she wasn't exactly sure. Shadowed lighting was such that she couldn't see his face

A door handle rattled.

He straightened from his slouched position in the sagging chair and placed the tea cup on the floor.

Daisy stiffened into a paralyzed pose and held her breath.

The front door squealed.

Phew.

Maybe it was Mrs. Brown.

Obviously distracted, the man turned his attention from Daisy's position and rose. "Who's there?" He mumbled.

An autumn breeze swirled around her ankles. The musty, pungent stench from years of accumulated papers and who-knew-what-else that lived beneath the stacks penetrated Daisy's tight space. Her nose twitched. A sneeze threatened. She pinched her nostrils and her cheeks puffed.

"Only me," The female-sounding person answered. "Brought the fine jewelry and paintings we'd kept at Miry. Should be one more run. Then we'll be finished.

"It's nearly eight. We need to move faster."

The two converged in the kitchen out of Daisy's sight.

With their backs towards her, they chatted about where to hide their stolen possessions in the house.

Surely Mrs. Brown would notice the added stuff when she returned. Daisy had imagined the police thought Mrs. Brown was involved with the robberies with all the stuff in her house. But, it was obvious it had been a set-up by these vandals.

Daisy peered out from the dark corner.

With the house invaders preoccupied this might be her only chance to escape.

She tiptoed past the chair, careful not to hit the teacup on the floor, around the television stand, towers of magazines and made it to the door leading to the master bedroom.

"When Brown gets back," the man said, "we'll

wait until she's gone out with that annoying pug of hers. Then we'll take this outta here and move on. We've stolen all we can from Worlingburgh."

"I think we're taking a chance stashing it in this place. What if that prying American comes over or looks out the window? She sticks her nose into others' business more than most. We gave her quite a scare last night, didn't we?" The female cackled again —the sound harsh and grating.

"Americans are a loud and nosey lot. I'll take care of her if she gets in the way." The man's tone resembled a creepy Anthony Hopkins in *The Silence of the Lambs* that sent a quiver along Daisy's neckline. She stopped mid-step and waited.

"Like you did George? Then shoved him in the freezer." The other sounded alarmed and less self-assured, as if frightened by her companion.

Daisy continued into the master bedroom and hid behind the door. Who could George be? The knifed man at Number Ten? If she could record what they were saying on her phone she'd have solid evidence about the death and robberies.

"He 'ad it coming to 'im. And, you will too if you don't keep your trap shut. He got in the way. That's all."

Despite the fact Daisy's knee pulsated with pain down to the top of her foot and up the thigh, her throat parched as the Sahara and she was scared witless, it would be now or never to prove her worth as a sleuth.

Decker would be livid if he knew what she'd been up to. Bless his heart, he wanted so much to help and protect her. In spite of Daisy's hammering heartbeat and sweaty palms, she sensed Decker was with her in spirit. But, she'd have to face his wrath for acting so carelessly, that was for sure.

Daisy snuggled further behind the door and next to the balled-up clothing where the tabby had escaped.

She pulled her phone halfway out of the coat pocket to avoid its light being seen. The battery showed twenty percent. Hopefully those two would repeat what had been said, but if nothing else she could catch them in the act of bringing things into the house.

"What about back in here? Think it's a bedroom," The man apparently headed in her direction as his voice grew louder.

She was trapped. There'd be no escaping now.

He stepped further into the room. "What a tip. How does the old lady live like this? My girlfriend would have a fit if she had to put up with such a dump."

Daisy watched him through the opening above the hinge on the doorframe and switched on the phone's recorder. This would be the perfect time to catch them in the act.

"Did you hear that?" He flicked on the wall switch. Daisy was instantly half-bathed in light.

The woman joined him. "What's the matter?"

"I heard something."

She crouched behind the pile and covered her head with a tattered woolen sweater. The thing made her itchy even before it hit her skin. Was it filled with fleas? She lifted a small corner and watched their feet as they moved further inside.

"I'm sure someone's in here."

Meow. Meow.

From under the sweater, Daisy watched the black cat scamper out from beneath the bed, stand its ground and hiss at the invaders. Another cat, grey with white paws emerged from nowhere. How many animals did Mrs. Wendy Brown actually own?

The man stomped his foot.

The animals scattered out of sight.

"It's just some crazy moggies. Let's put the stash in another room. Who knows what else is hiding in here."

The pair left and Daisy exhaled, her body going limp. Good thing she was already close to the floor, or she might have collapsed with relief. Right now, all she wanted was for them to be gone for good.

She tried not to scratch the burning skin around

her neck and face. Hives might turn out to be her next nemesis.

Maybe it would be best to forget recording these two criminals. If she could just take a picture surely that would suffice in a court of law.

Daisy moved stealthily back into the sitting room as the set of thieves went out the front and carried armfuls of things through the kitchen and into an adjoining room. A long drape over the window would be a perfect place for her to watch without being seen.

Making sure the phone was on silent and the flash off, she aimed the camera and took a burst of pictures as they entered with another load. Unfortunately, their backs faced her. She'd have to wait for them to do another run to their vehicle and snap a shot as the reentered.

When they disappeared outside, she prepared her view to take the perfect picture.

One of the two returned.

Where had the other gone?

The man grabbed her arm and yanked her out from behind the curtain. "Caught ya. I knew someone was in here."

CHAPTER 24

*D*aisy struggled against Postman Robert's tight clasp.

Part of her didn't want to believe it was him. Especially for Rosemary's sake. Her friend had been beguiled by this soft-spoken, unassuming chap who'd turned out to be a royal creep. Another man betrayed Rosemary's affections not long ago, and it broke Daisy's heart.

She fought and squealed like a pig trying to get free.

"Stop fighting. And stop making that noise." He shook her until Daisy almost crumbled to the floor. She forced herself to stay upright. The least she could do was maintain any ounce of dignity left.

"Let me go!"

Robert tightened his grip. "Not a chance. You should've minded your own business."

"How could you do this to others?"

He narrowed his eyes and licked his lips. "Easy."

"People trusted you with their mail and packages. Then you went into their homes knowing full well when they aren't around and took what doesn't belong to you."

"It's called progressive thinking. Or you could say I'm a modern Robin Hood. Taking from the rich to give to the poor. The poor, being me."

"But, you stole from innocent folks." How long could she talk and try to stall this idiot from doing her harm?

"What's it to you?" Robert dragged Daisy by the arm into the center of the sitting room. Bright morning beams penetrated the room and revealed massive amounts of floating dust particles. A sneeze threatened again. But fear quickly snuffed the sensation.

She growled through clenched teeth. "Trust me, you won't get away with this. You'll be found out."

"You're such a fool. Once we take care of you, no one will ever know."

"I told friends I thought you were involved." Lying to a devil like Robert was surely a forgivable offense.

"Why don't I believe you?" He snarled.

"What's this?" The female entered from the other part of the house. Daisy thought she had recognized the voice—the Marine-sounding woman from the bakery who'd spoken about the victim in Number Ten being knifed. It was now apparent she'd been there when Robert had done the dirty dead. "I see you found the snoop."

"Told you I heard something."

"What are you going to do with her?" The Marine stood at attention in the doorway. Daisy couldn't make out whether she was encouraging or questioning Robert.

"What da ya think?"

"Is it necessary?" Although the woman appeared to be physically strong, she seemed to shrivel under Robert's gaze.

"Don't you worry about her. Finish bringing the stuff into the house. Who knows when Brown will return?"

The woman turned and exited without another word.

"Now what to do with you?" He sneered at Daisy.

"You don't have to do anything with me. I promise not to say anything."

"Yeah, right. You already said you'd told others. Besides, who'd miss Daisy McFarland? You live alone and don't have many friends. I know everything there is to know about everyone in the village. Including you. You're a nobody."

More than anything, Daisy hated being spoken to like this. She'd had enough as a teacher. Mustering up a thin dose of courage, she used her good leg and thrust a knee where it hurt men the most.

His face a horrible grimace, Robert released his grip, curled over at the waist and gagged. "You hag."

Daisy bolted away as quick as she could only to trip over a stack of papers. Years of Daily Mail tumbled over and knocked her down.

Robert groaned, but managed to reach Daisy and jerk her up onto her feet. He hauled her to the sagging chair and threw her into it. "If you move, I'll take care of you like I did George."

"Come in here, Marge." Robert yelled to the woman as she entered the house.

"What?" Marge barked. Her patience obviously wearing thin.

"Keep an eye on Miss McFarland. I need to take care of something." He hobbled away, obviously still in pain. "I'll be right back."

"Why are you doing this?" Daisy sat upright and fought the urge to cry. Tears would do her no good against this formidable woman.

"Shut up." Marine paced back and forth in front of Daisy. A warrior on patrol duty.

Daisy slumped back and softened her tone. "It's

obvious he's taking advantage of you. Do you really think he'll let you go when he's finished? You're a liability to him. After all, you saw him murder George."

The woman stopped in front of the chair. "How do you know that?"

"I overheard you. When you were in there." She nodded in the direction of the bedroom. "And in the bakery yesterday."

"You really are a meddler. Why'd ya have to get your nose into something that doesn't concern you?"

"Oh, but it does. I'm worried about my friends. And I'm concerned for you, Marge." Daisy knew very well the signs of insecurity. Of wanting to belong and doing anything to be accepted.

The woman threw her head back and laughed. "Please."

"Look. You don't have to do this. That man's dangerous. I don't know what he's promised, but I'm sure there will be no walking away from this unscathed."

The harsh lines on Marge's face softened, and she dropped the fisted hands resting on her hips. "I suppose you're right."

Daisy moved to the edge of the chair and looked up at her guard. "You and I could escape right now. Once we're outta here, we can go to the police together. We can tell them how Robert came up with this scheme. I'm sure they'll be more lenient if you confess."

The woman looked over her shoulder and back at Daisy. She leaned at the waist and whispered. "Do you really think you could get out of here? He's roughed you up pretty good, plus it looks like you've got a bum leg."

"We could try."

Robert returned, his cheeks flamed. "What are you two whispering about?"

"Nothing." Marge shuffled sideways from Daisy.

"It's now or never to take care of Miss McFarland. We've run out of time and she's run out of luck."

CHAPTER 25

*D*aisy rubbed her arm, hit a tender spot, and flinched. Robert had gripped it so hard, there'd have to be a large black-and-blue mark, if she actually lived long enough to see it.

Between a bad knee, itching and sneezing from the bugs and dust, plus a smarting arm and bruised ego, Daisy sank further into the filthy chair and moaned. Robert was right. Only he left something out in his assessment about Daisy being a nobody. She was also a very silly woman. One of these days she might get a brain like the Wizard of Oz scarecrow and not go into dangerous situations without letting others know.

"Let's get this over with." Robert grumbled to Marge in the kitchen while keeping an eye on Daisy and discussed how best to get rid of their prisoner without leaving a trace. The woman towered over him by several inches, yet he bossed her like she was a subordinate troop.

"I told you. I'll take care of her," Marge said.

"You try and act tough, but you don't have the courage." The postman seemed to be losing patience with his partner and his voice escalated as he moved in Daisy's direction.

Marge grabbed his forearm and forced him to face her as they stood in the doorway. "Look, didn't you say you were going to do your route today as usual?" she asked, her softening tone suggesting a shift in tactics.

"Plans have to be adjusted. McFarland altered our perfect scheme and she's going to pay for it."

"But if I get rid of her, why do you have to change the plan? This way no one will think you're involved. You can quietly leave your job once we've got the goods in another place and we can move on."

A long pause punctured the conversation, as Robert apparently considered Marge's suggestion. Was the marine trying to give Daisy time to escape? Or should she wait it out in case the woman persuaded the postman to let her deal with the situation?

Could Daisy trust Marge with her life? Or had she been toying with her earlier?

Robert hesitated. "I don't know. You cringed like a baby when George had to be done away with."

"That was different. I wasn't expecting it. But, like you said. He was a liability. He'd have blown the whistle on us."

The two entered the sitting room and approached Daisy.

If a face could resemble a Halloween mask, Marge's full, black-arched brows and bulging golf-ball-sized eyeballs would be the perfect disguise for someone trying to frighten others. Robert's look mirrored the marine's with evil flickering from his beady eyes, and a long lock of hair traveling down his forehead that added to the fiendish appearance.

"You're sure you can do this?" Robert asked.

Marge's tone turned harsh and commanding. "I'm telling ya. I'll take care of this cow. Probably better than you could. Believe me, you won't be disappointed."

Daisy winced and crossed her arms in front of her face as the two approached the chair.

Robert finally gave in. "Fine. I've got to get my uniform and vehicle. Text when you're done here. But, hurry it up. Brown's bound to come back soon."

Daisy lifted an arm and peeked out.

The postman left and Marge watched him depart.

"Whew. Thank you. That was close. Now we can get out of here." Daisy started to get up.

"What are you going on about?" Marge snarled.

"I thought...you...were...going to the police station with me and turn yourself in."

Her eyes narrowed. "I didn't say any such thing."

Daisy retreated back into the seat. "What...what are you going to do to me?"

"I'm thinking. Don't make this any more difficult than it has to be."

Robert peered around the kitchen corner. He hadn't left after all. Had he been testing Marge and she knew it? "I'm outta here. Make it quick."

The marine gave him a half-salute as the door slammed shut. "You idiot. You almost got both of us killed. What were you thinking?"

"I didn't know he was still in the house."

"He's no fool. I knew he'd be hiding, waiting to make sure I did his dirty work."

"Should we leave by the back?"

"I'm not sure I trust you. How do I know you'll back me up?"

Daisy stood. "Look. I'm tired, bruised and ready to go home. Are you going to join me or stick with that loser? He murdered George and you're the eyewitness. It's now or never to decide."

Marge hung her head and released a long sighed. "I'm tired too." When she looked up, her golf-ball eyes brimmed with tears. "That swine used me and my George. I had to act like I agreed with the pig or he'd have killed me, too. George wasn't anything special, but he was special to me. We were going to be together when this was all over."

"Let's go then. Before Robert changes his mind and comes back."

Marge guided Daisy through the hallway towards the master bedroom and turned left. "I noticed there was a backdoor through here, but it's gonna take some doing to get out. We can't chance going out the front."

"Once we're out of here, we can go to my house and then I'll drive us to the station."

Tossing aside books, clothing, and tons of bric-a-brac, some broken into smaller pieces that could cut if they weren't careful, they managed to dig a narrow opening to the door.

"Wait." Marge whispered as Daisy reached for the handle.

"What is it?"

"He might be waiting out there. The man's devious and might've figured out what we're up to."

Daisy pulled out her phone. "Let me text my friends to come over. They'll help us." She groaned. "Oh, no. The battery. It's dead." Daisy turned to Marge. "Wait, don't you have a phone?"

"It's out in the kitchen. Do we want to take the

time for me to go back and get it? It's taken so long to get through this mess. Or should we take a chance and leave?"

Daisy paused a few seconds and placed her hand on the knob. "Let's get out of here. Now."

CHAPTER 26

*B*rilliant sunlight hit Daisy and Marge as they left the house, moved through the side yard and out the rear gate.

"Wow. That's bright." Daisy kept her voice down. Who knew where Robert might be?

She shaded her eyes with a cupped hand while they stood beside the bins and waited until her eyes adjusted.

"It's wonderful to be out in fresh air, isn't it?" Daisy always felt rejuvenated when fall colors burst out on the tips of leaves and smells of autumn floated on a breeze. Right this moment, she was never more thankful to be alive with that the villainous postman long gone. Or was he?

"George liked fall." Marge inhaled and let out a

long sigh. "I guess we'd better get this over with and head to the station."

Bushes rustled on Daisy's left. She gasped.

Robert pounced out from behind the bins. He blocked them—his arms outstretched, crouching as if ready to tackle. "You're heading somewhere. But, it's not to the station. It's straight to you-know-where."

Daisy hid behind Marge and trembled at the man's sheer presence. "What are you doing here?"

He ignored Daisy and barked at the marine. "I knew you were rotten. You're a traitor just like that imbecile, George."

"He wasn't an imbecile." Marge recoiled her right arm, rolled her hand into a tight fist and slammed Robert square in the face. He fell flat on his back and held his nose. Instantly, he curled into a fetal position and rolled back and forth in agony, blood streaming from between his fingers and down his chin.

Daisy came out from behind Marge, and they palmed a high-five. "Whoa. You clobbered him. I'm sure this'll help with your defense, too. Somehow, we need to get him tied up."

"I think we can help with that." Decker and Mark ran in tandem across the lawn that stretched between the back of Daisy's and Mrs. Brown's.

"How'd you find me?" Daisy rushed into Decker's

arms while Mark yanked Robert up by the scruff of his neck.

"You need to learn how to lock up your house, Miss Daisy." Mark grasped the postman's hands tightly behind the man's back. "Your front door was unlocked."

Decker held Daisy at arm's length as if assessing her condition. "We both showed up at your house at the same time—"

"When we saw the pets were wandering the house," Mark said, finishing Decker's sentence, "we knew something had to be up. Especially since Treacle was there."

"I called the station and found out Mrs. Wendy Brown had been held overnight for psychological testing. We put two and two together and figured you might've gone over to her place." Decker added.

"Now why would you think that?" Daisy offered a weak smile.

The deepened dimple and twinkle in Decker's eyes spoke volumes. He seemed to know her better than she'd realized.

Mark nodded at Decker. "He's a good policeman to have around when you need one."

After Decker scrutinized Daisy once more, as though to make sure she could manage on her own, he took Marge tightly by the arm to ward off any idea she might have to bolt. "Thanks, Mark. It was a team effort. You made some of your own calls that helped."

Like Pillow and Treacle, these two men seemed to realize they weren't enemies and could possibly be friends.

"There you are." Rosemary came running from her house towards Daisy, grabbed and hugged her. "You crazy lady. What've you been up to?"

They released each other and Daisy shrugged. "You know me. Always getting into trouble. Sorry about your most recent beau." She pointed in Robert's direction. "Turns out he's a murderer."

Her friend shrugged. "I've got the worst taste in men. I'm just thankful you're okay."

A hint of sadness in Rosemary's eyes contradicted her nonchalant response. The revelation of a potential love interest turning out to be a rogue had stung, and Daisy's heart went out to her.

"Weren't we supposed to help you find these thieves?" Mark asked as the troupe moved away from Mrs. Brown's house and headed towards Daisy's.

"Yeah. We were supposed to do this together," Decker said.

Daisy stopped dead in her tracks as they reached halfway to her house. "Wait a second. I forgot to check out something." She turned around and hobbled back towards Mrs. Brown's.

Rosemary rushed along beside her. "You aren't going anywhere without me for quite some time. Looks like you can hardly walk. And what's happened to your arm?"

"I'll be okay." Daisy limped to the gate.

"Besides, what do you need to do that's so urgent?"

"Check out what she's hiding in her bins. I'm working on a novel, remember? I need to find out what my antagonist is up to."

Daisy slowly lifted the lid and chuckled. "Well, I'll be"

"What is it?"

"I'd been so curious to know what Brown had in here. I thought it might've been tools of torture or remnants of thievery that she'd been trying to hide. I've never been so wrong about someone as I have about her."

Rosemary joined Daisy and looked inside. "What in the world?"

Normally used for compost, it was filled with several large bags of cat food and litter. "I guess Mrs. Wendy Brown didn't want her neighbors to know how many felines she owned. And believe me, she owns plenty. This was probably the only place free to store the food."

"How strange." Rosemary's eyebrow lifted.

Daisy held her side and laughed. "Mrs. Brown is

no criminal. All along, it's just been about a plethora of cats." And most likely cats having an amorous interlude could explain the strange "like-someone-being-murdered" noises that rocked the neighborhood.

Pillow would definitely enjoy the tale.

"I'M FINE, REALLY." At last, Daisy could rest. Rosemary pampered her as if she were an invalid, tucking a blanket around Daisy's legs as she stretched out on the sofa. After making sure Pillow and Treacle were well taken care of, going to the police station to deliver Robert and Marge, giving a statement about what had happened and handing over the key to Number Ten, she felt somewhat incapacitated. Pillow had planted herself on the sofa's arm behind her head and stood guard while Treacle slept by her feet.

"Here's your tea, madam." Mark carried out a tray with mugs, a pot and biscuits for a party of four and began to "play mother" as the British would say about the one responsible for serving others.

"Rosemary brought over an adjustable tray on wheels to hold your computer should you be inspired while you recover." Decker slid the trolley beside the sofa and placed Daisy's full cup and a plate of McVities within easy reach.

Her friend, holding the boxed security cameras that would be mounted in due time, smiled and winked at her as the men vied for Daisy's attention.

The three stood in a row in front of her. Hear no evil, see no evil, speak no evil. Robert had been so wrong about her being a nobody. These friends accepted her for who she was and never reprimanded or spoke evil against her. She was indeed a blessed woman whose home was filled to the brim with friends and her heart wanted to burst with pride.

Meow. Meow.

Pillow echoed Daisy's joy.

THE END